QUIET REVISIONS

KIRSTEN GETER

ISBN 13: 978-0-9794032-3-1
ISBN10: 0-9794032-3-5

DEDICATION

For my heart in human forms: my husband Rommel, my children, Jasmine and Bryson, my family, blood and spirit, and all my loved ones.

CONTENTS

PREFACE

Thinking of our time together has sent my mind
On a journey to what could be
To new heights of possibilities
I've been thinking on what could transpire between us
That is, if you let your guard down and trust
That what I say is real

I think deep down you know you feel this
But you keep backing away from the shining that draws
your spirit near my own
I'll admit it
You've got me gone on thoughts of spending time in your
presence I think about your essence
Wishing to feel it within my being again until the sunrises
Our bodies speaking in unspoken languages
Thinking about how it would be to sit and watch TV all
day in bed
With your chest being a pillow for my head
Or your head resting on my thighs and looking into deep
eyes

I've been thinking
You're unlike anyone I've been with before
Got my mind open, heart beating
Got me sitting home hoping you'll call
I think I am on the brink of falling for you
But too soon to fall
So I'll simply say that I've simply thought it
Yeah I've been thinking about falling for you

But I think I'll wait
Find out what you want to do
Uncertain in this game of chance
Not sure if it's real or some game of secret romance

With no real chance of growing into something real
So I hold back what I really want,
but can't change how I feel
So real, so gone, so blown on thoughts of you
I like the way I feel in your in your space
The smile that pours from my face
Just from the sound of your voice on the other end of my
phone

I've been thinking
I'm ready to show you my world
if you are willing to share yours with me too
Unlike any you've known before

I can promise you this
From my intellect, to my confidence, to the softness of
each kiss
I can show you things that you can dream of in time,
From good music, to a love of books, some nice full
bodied
wines. . .

Let me in and I'll shine—some light into your world
This is a special brew that I offer with libations of
spirituality,
possibility, and truth
I've been thinking that I have some things to share with
you
That is if you have the time

1 VIRGIN ON THE MIC

Sitting in the back of the room, Yakini flips through her papers unsure what she was going to perform. With the lights so dim, it seems it would be difficult to know just which work she's looking at. But no, she knows each one by heart. Recognizing a word or two in the middle of the page allows her to know exactly which piece she had in hand. No one else seems to have papers on stage.

The performers here are wonderful – energetic, emotional, moving, but at times redundant in their content. Sexual conquests usually spill from the lips of the smooth brother, revolutionary incites from the sister with the dread extensions, I-can't-find-a-good-man-blues from the sister in the spandex dress that is cut just below her plump derriere. Yet, their stage presence makes them shine on stage. They bring dramatic life to their works, sing interludes, or simply bring so much passion out of their works that no matter how simplistic the words, they seem to create innovative definitions.

Yakini knows her words are sound, honest, pure, and moving. But as it is, she is a pen and paper, sit down and think, meditate and flow poet. Although not graceful on the mic, too shy to look at the audience for long periods of time, and a bit of shakiness in her voice, her words resound, move, enlighten, and inspire. Finally, she hears someone announcing her, or at least attempting to pronounce her name.

Making her way to the stage, she wishes she had pushed herself to memorize one of her works. Spoken word nights are her chance to let someone other than herself hear her works. However, they never end up the way she dreams them because her shyness makes her unable to just get up there and say it the way she felt it when she wrote it down. Many times, she says she not going to do it again, get on that stage and attempt to gain an audience, but then more words invade her mind, make their way to the page, and she had to let someone hear them. Once on stage, she looks down at the piece of paper and clears her throat,

"Peace and blessings room, this piece is new. Well, we often hear love poems, but this one's a special request from a friend, a lover of music who asked me to write out his desires for the feel of music in his ears from a woman's point of view with music being the man created solely for to her. Hopefully hearing this one will make you think of a day when you heard your song, that song that makes you relax, unwind, and smile from the first note."

Captivating blue and yellow hues surround me
As I am awed by your beautiful curves and sharp angles
Entanglement of emotions and colors fill my mind as I attempt
To find my place within your space
I can trace your fluid movements and your abrupt breaks
As I bask in your presence, I am soothed by your poetics
Your energy induces my spirit to think of majestic scenes
Our intimate moments spent as I relax from my day
Range from romantic interludes played out in stereo
To blues belted in a sad contra-alto by a needle drawn along a groove

Feeling like a lady for the day as Lady Day swoons in my ear
Elevated so high, I believe I am able fly up how high the moon is
At times, I write out my desires to you in our secret language
That is filled with pauses and scribbles and circles and lines
Written in a kind of cryptic penmanship
And each syllable has a million emotions swirling and intermingling in it
That create one perfect note that I seal with a kiss
And place under your pillow
So, they can be realized in your dreams
And I pray these words somehow will become authentic scenes
Caused purely by your love for me
You have power to invoke my sheer thoughts to become sound statements
Captivating blue and yellow hues surround me
As I am awed by your beautiful curves and sharp angles
Entanglement of emotions and colors fill my mind as I attempt to find my place within your space
I can trace your fluid movements and your abrupt breaks
As I bask in your presence, I am soothed by your poetics

It is over; the crowd claps. I love Wednesday nights here at Harmony. I always know that no matter if I stumble over my words or have to restart my reading the people always show the poet on stage love. They reciprocate the energy back to their own, back to the ones telling their stories. This love is what calls me back here in a bundle of nerves to read on the mic.

The audience, they give thanks to those painting pictures of their lives, their loves, their desires through words. Here on this night, they remind me that I'm a storyteller, an acapella griot, weaving together history, prophesy, enchantment, and love to create a story of their ancestry, legend, strength.

Here on this stage I remind them of their childhood games, their school dances, first loves, wrong loves, heart breaks, love affairs, remind them of the time before they were even conceived. I narrate their stories. Nights here help to remind me that although I cannot sway and contort my voice into fanciful characters, that my words are still art that I speak to a thirsting audience. Weekly I shower down refreshing dew of remembrance that their parched minds need; each line a drop of black rain helping to overcome the droughts caused by our eradication from American history. I guess some may think I am making this poetry thing sound too important, but then they could be wrong.

Going back to my seat, I smile at the people as I maneuver my way back to my table. The girl with the locs pulled into a high ponytail, accentuating her high cheekbones and slanted eyes, shakes her head, closes her eyes, and just moans "hmmm hmmm hmmm." This reminds me that I, Yakini Johnson, am a poet. Not because someone could find the symbolism, feel the rhythm, point out a rhyme scheme, or even count the meter. Oh no, just a moan and a shake of the head tells me that this sista felt me. Felt my words in her soul and could find no words to tell me, only a shake of her head.

Back at my table, my girl squeezes my arm. Sister love is brilliant when it is real. That kind of love that women share that has no strings attached, not done out of necessity, obligation, or pity, but just because. Because we reflect each other in our smiles, tears, and laughter.

"That was great girl. I really liked that one"

"NaNa, look behind you to your left at the one with the locs with the linen shirt on." She pointed to a beautiful brother with hair screamed out to Yakini to come and play.

"Looks like your type. Go say something to him, ask him how he liked the poem."

Now after eleven years of friendship Naomi knows there

is no way that I am going to go over there and just talk to this brother. Now when I was young and "hot" (as my Auntie would say), I would have been over there in a second handing him my number, but not now. Time teaches many things, patience, etiquette, and decorum. I look at him and smile.

"If he's interested, he'll come over. As my daddy told me, times may have changed, but men have not. If a man sees something he wants, he won't wait for it to come to him. He'll pursue. It's his nature."

But I know that in the times that we live in, the prey has formed a predatory nature and completely screwed the entire hunt issue, but I stay in my seat, order a glass of merlot, and continue to talk to my girl glancing in his direction every so often. Three more poets have gone, and the vibe is wonderful tonight. This room is beautiful with tables lit by a single candle, hard wood floors, and the band is playing the sweetest mix of jazz and funk ever heard.

The host announces another poet, "Ok, we finally have gotten to a brother on the list of poets tonight. Being the first man to read tonight, let's show him some love room. Mr. Kyle Niane."

The brother with the locs and the linen shirt stands up, grabs a small notebook, smiles at me, and walks to the stage. Now this isn't "Love Jones" and I am not Nina, so he didn't do a poem for me when he got on stage.

Instead, he seemed to step into my mind, access my beliefs, and divulge them to the room as if they were his own.

"Alright room, how y'all doing tonight? This piece is one I wrote a while back and for some reason I felt it needed to be read. Everyone in here has a mission, not just the poets, singers, and artists, but each of us has a calling that drives us to do what we do. This piece sums up why I write, why I read, why I have no choice but to love words, the telling of these words, and their tellers.

Modern Day Griot

I am a griot,
Ancestor of those African vessels of speech
Who held in their hearts the art of expressive speaking,
Recording the past in poetry
Allowing their people a history,
Orally telling of their foundation,
Creation of their nations,
Wars, tribes, fights,
Despite Western insight that oral history is faulty
The shaman continue to sing of the memory of Mankind

Recapture their legends in rhyme, scatted, and Swooned
As old as time, before the creation of paper and pen,
History's haven when all else was forbidden
Before able to grasp the pen, steal the paper, our history was able to withstand this period of mass incarceration
See those who entrapped those ebony skinned men knew not
That a griot is not simply an occupation
But is passed through blood lines for generations
As the ships navigated seas,
In the minds of the shaman it was history
That grew slowly grew, cultivated by their Imaginations
Like cotton by the red clay of the south
History budded in beautiful flowers of song
Unseen to naked eyes but told through legendary Stories
Made to seem childlike
From Iyadola's babies to Africans who take flight,

Gullah slaves with power to take wing and fly
home,
Master said it was a lie a trick of the light,
But Overseer told it; the boy didn't have time to run,
Jumped on his hoe and flew on home,
See he came from a people with wings black as coal,
Flapping up against the blue African sky,
But on the ship many got sick of the motion and forgot
how to fly
Yes, some have since forgot about flying
And don't remember they can fly,
But a griot like me knows of those who came across
the sea
Shed their wings, but kept their secret magic in land of
Slavery
Tales spread in bedtime stories
Of briar rabbit with his tar baby,
Legends,
Myths,
Tales spreading history,
Carried on clear through to dramatist like Willis
Richardson in 1923,
On to his following playwrights Charles Gardone,
Charles Fuller and on
To August Wilson and Anna Deaver Smith's telling of
our 1992 riotous
history
The legends kept moving past stage into new variety,
Going past the theater morphing into fiction,
History still told beneath the plots hidden
Found in the minds of Richard Wright, Ralph Ellison,
James Baldwin further still to Toni Morrison,
Ishmael Reed, Alice Walker, and Terry McMillan
Griots passed also to poets like Jupiter Harmon,
Phyllis Wheatley and George Horton,
Down to Paul Lawrence Dunbar after the Civil War,
The flow of the griot continued to the Renaissance in

Harlem,
To poets such as Langston
Hughes, Claude McKay, Countee Cullen,
And James
Weldon
Johnson
Continued on this voyage to spread the words,
History,
Legends, Tales of their ancestry, the griot kept flowing
From
Gwendolyn Brooks to Rita Dover
Onto to Sonja Sanchez, Margret Walker,
And Nikki Giovanni,

Ah see,
The griot river of knowledge coasted steadily, from the coast of the Ivory
Sea,

Onto slave ship into slavery,
Through emancipation,
Past the rebuilding of our nation,
It flowed through the freedom ride,
Civil rights movement plights,
It continued on it voyage stopping in the voices of
Many
Continued
Its way
Until it found

Me. . .
For see, I am a griot,
Sent to heal my nation,
Tell of not just our origin, but of our current situation,
In my blood flows that of a noble craftsman who told of a wonderful past,

Things that outlast paper and pen
See the soul of the poet is within the words, that last forever once spoken,
Live in those, to whom it was said,
The minds of those to whom the lines were read
I am griot
Getting fancy with expressions
Expanding my lexicon to include my
People's missions and our past
Out last any that comes with only a
Textbook and facts,
For it is within the blood of griot, that the history
Is waxed, sealed and secure
Able to endure all that comes to pass
I am a poet,
A storyteller,
A narrator of tales for my voiceless community,
I am the modern day, griot.

I realize he has no idea why I am smiling at him as if he is speaking solely to me, but for a moment, it feels like this indeed is the moment that Darius reads "A Blues for Nina," and he knows he has written out a poem telling some dark secret we shared in another lifetime. He walks back toward his table and grabs his brown suede shoulder bag.

Dag, I should've spoken to him. At least introduced myself, ah well, it's too late now. I look back to the stage; the host is doing one of his own pieces while the band plays a bluesy performance behind him softly. I close my eyes, take a sip, and feel the notes. Then a hand on my shoulder, I turn and see the linen shirt.

"Excuse me; can I talk to you out in the courtyard for a few minutes?"

I tell Naomi that I'll be right back. I follow the linen shirt, all the while fixating on the beautiful locs that hang on the shoulders of coffee colored linen cloth. Once outside, the air is nice.

"I wanted to tell you that I was really feeling your words in there. By the way, I'm Kyle. "

"Same to you—your words were beautiful. So when did you know that you were a griot?"

He smiles and looks down – cute kind of introverted look, like when you're thinking of something funny that happened but no one around you knows the story so you just close your eyes and smile to yourself – well one of those smiles is what he does when I ask him that.

"Nice for a sister to ask me that and not what is a griot."

"Nice for a brother to mention some sisters in his poems as story tellers and not just escapades."

We both kind of take a deep breath and smile. Now, I am not sure if I am just assuming, not wanting to assume because we all know the kind of mess that usually makes, but I think he is feeling more than my poetry.

"By the way what was your name again? I didn't quite catch it when Solomon announced you."

"Oh yeah, I heard him stumble through my name. Seems like as many times as I have come here, he would remember it by now. I'm Yakini."

"Do you come here often, seems I would have noticed you by now."

"Well I've been in a few times on and off over the last couple of months. I've been looking for a good spot to read.

"Oh, so you're new to this. I wouldn't have thought so."

Yakini looks down and smiles. She was somewhat shy although she hid it well usually, "Well thanks. I'm growing with it."

"The name, Yakini, interesting is there meaning behind it or just— " He hoped she didn't think he was being impolite, "I'm sorry, that was rude of me."

"No, it is fine. It means truth."

His eyes close again and that smile appears on his lips. Well actually, it begins in the closing of the eyelids, slips down into the bowing of his head, and like a dawning sun, it just slowly rises upward until his lips slightly curve, part slightly, and the smile is as phenomenal as the sun.

"Truth, I like that. Well Mrs. Truth, I guess I need to get home, work in the morning."

"Actually, it is Miss. Miss. Johnson. I hope you have a nice night Mr. Niane. I remembered from Solomon's introduction of you earlier."

I walked away from Kyle that night smiling. Not having exchanged numbers or even having set up a time to meet again, I walked away knowing that we'd definitely see one another again.

2 HARMONY OF SOULS

Word Power

Power of Words shapes reality
Create space effect the pace of progress
Words that test the boundaries press the walls
Correct the flaws
Words scrawled on building and train cars
Intended to reach far but instead viewed as a scar to the naked beauty of
metal and concrete
Meant to speak to minds and share histories
Untold in class
Obituaries for those unnamed in the Times
Personal headlines inscribed on schoolyard bricks with cans of paint and
energy to climb
To scale a way to tell the tales not told in nursery rhymes
Power of Words to be heard over radio waves
Break bonds of those enslaved by monetary lyrics
Prosperous to be replaced with the prophetic
Prolific

Where the telling of raunchy escapades is replaced with unions made
Foundations laid and respect paid to those who hold the conception of
future nations between thighs
Not simply created to induce brothers to imagine the rhythm of a possible
midnight ride
Prophetic powerful Words that spread new realities of black nationality
Creation of economic stability by the power
Of the Word to spread truth

Sitting at his desk with papers sprawled over every inch and facing in every possible direction, Kyle thought over the course he was to instruct this semester. This was his first semester teaching the course on African Diaspora Literature, and it was not quite as simple as he had assumed.

Actually, this was the first semester anyone at his university had taught this course. He had initially gone to the head of his English department, Mr. Garner, with a proposal for a course of African-American literature, which Kyle was appalled to find they did not have when he accepted his position at the university. It was amazing that in this time there were still institutions in the academic world that did not consider African-American writing as having literary importance. Of course, there are the few who have been embraced into the cannon, the few who have been deemed worthy, but the masses of literature produced by our people are disregarded as simply forms of entertainment, fluff, or better yet "nice." These were the very thoughts that propelled Kyle to reconsider his limited course on only African-American Literature.

He knew that the novel, a European invention, was not only sheltered from the fingers of the African-American writer, but all those of the Diaspora. Those minority writers, third-world country writers, who had also been marginalized in the literary world, became the focus of his proposal.

The ideas began pouring as he composed his class description. The notes he had scribbled all were on the premise of the ancestors of a people estranged from their place of origin by forceful means writing about a culture, which was a hybrid of two nations, two cultures, several languages. Yet it was the blurred ethnicities, their loss of certainty of their lineage and their constant desire to recreate a history through literature that pushed Kyle to see that his initial vision was too narrow and needed to be expanded to include more.

The course grew into a theory instead that even removed by distance, language, and centuries, the descendants of the Diaspora, these Diasporic authors, still shared some common bonds through their histories, thoughts, ideals, and words—no matter in which language they were expressed.

He had discovered the thread. Well actually, he had forced himself to find something that connected the writers in the way he proposed. The collection he composed was filled with novels with an essence of defiance and rebellion, but searching for a way to find acceptance of self, self-evaluation, and the love of their hybridism in their new native lands. He smiled as he ended his reading list with works that showed these descendants of the Diaspora finally recognizing their authentic self and not seeing their transformation simply as surrender to assimilation. This acceptance inspired Kyle to continue his notes. The final light at the end of the tunnel that affirmed that this disjoined family somehow had found a way to love its past, presents, and anticipate a future in a new home, no longer viewed only as their holding place. He wrote on the ability for a people initially seized for their physical worth that were judged to be a people abused, trained, and broken to instead be a nation of nurtures, intellects, and healers. He wrote on the amazing story of unity prevailing even through their displacement and division. Beautiful lectures he composed telling of the up building of original cultures from the remnants of the past and the optimism for a future.

"Mr. Garner, here's a copy of the reading list, syllabus, and more detailed course description for the website and to the updated list of available Literature classes for the fall."

"Very well, Mr. Niane, it was coming down to the wire, and I honestly didn't think you would finish in time. I am glad you did, but I just didn't think you were so close to finishing when we last spoke on your progress."

"I see. Well, I think you will find the detailed description a little, let's say, different from my initial proposal. Now, I didn't completely change the idea for the course, but I did expand it to incorporate a wider range of writers."

"Is this still to be considered an African-American Literature course of some sort?"

"Well, not really. It is more so a course on writers of the Diaspora."

"I see. Interesting concept, but what will these 'descendant'-writers have in common besides their roots in slavery?"

"That is to be a part of the course, sir. This course will show the link that these writers share."

"Mr. Niane that is a bit presumptuous; don't you think?"

"Yes, but I think most of our courses here presume some things. Our Film as Literature class makes the presumption that a film can be viewed as a type of literature. Our course on Women writers presumes that women have reasons to write on specific topics and share some common bonds. So to answer you, yes it is presumptuous, but no more than anything else in the world of academia."

"Mr. Niane, you know the procedure. If wanted to change the class, it must first go through the correct persons."

"I thought that since this was my concept that I would be the correct person to make fine tuning adjustments. Now I have known many professors, including myself, who have chosen to change some aspects of a course that we were teaching. It has never been a problem before today."

"Not to sound arrogant, but I'm the decider in this case. Kyle, I'm disappointed in your rashness. I'll look over these plans and get back to you on the issue. Make an appointment with my secretary to come back Wednesday for my decision and we will see if this course will be offered at all this semester."

"Mr. Garner, I am sure. . ."

"That will be all Mr. Niane, Wednesday."

~~~~~~~~~~~~~

At Café Harmony, the gathering was thin tonight. Good. He wasn't really in the mood for crowds. Kyle tried to understand why Mr. Garner had reacted to the changes in the proposal the way that he did. Actually, he fought with the fact that sadly it wasn't odd. That's what bothered him. He knew where his school was located, but somehow took the liberal political conversations as a reflection on their personal beliefs. He knew that most of the professors there were not looking for a revolution, but he thought that they all would definitely join into one that had merit.

Kyle gazed into his glass while he thought over these things, "Mr. Garner confessed liberal, the consummate democrat who pushed diversity and advocated any training dealing with cultural affairs, unsure if my course is reasonable. How dare, he assumes to think he knows what connections I share to anyone. Democrat, liberal, reasonable, right, he is until I go outside his box of reason. He is so open-minded until I present an idea that seems to be a little too controversial for the university. How dare I use slavery in a course without using it to show how demeaning it was, how dare I show that no matter how brutal and horrific, it was a catalyst that created these intelligent, profound, and skilled writers. How dare me? No how dare he think he can tell me what my people have in
~~~~~~~~~~~~~

common."

"Kyle," Solomon was standing with his hand on Kyle's shoulder.

"Yeah."

"You were zoning for a moment there. I asked if you were reading tonight."

"Oh, nah. Not tonight. I haven't got a thing prepared to read. I just came for the energy. I need a jolt and there's no place like Harmony for a good soul jump."

"Alright, well I hope you'll be ready next week. Don't go on another poetic hiatus like you did for the last few months. You just got back into the scene and you know what the old people say, 'Use it, or lose it.' Don't lose your gift brother; it only lives when you share it."

Now Solomon was a brother who talked a great game about poetry, writing, and the mind state of writers. Yet in all honesty, his poetry was the typical inadequately duplicated Love Jones, finger snaps, commercialized to sell liquor and cars kind poetry – stale and expected. He was the archetypal black male poet spitting the same issues over and over in different phrases, rhythms, and tone. Really, there were about three topics he hit: sex, racism, and love, in that order. Now not saying these topics are not weighty and not saying these topics don't need to be talked about by talented writers, but, there comes a time when a poet, a real poet that doesn't simply rhyme and make generalized imagery, has to step back and think on things not so often discussed. And yes, there are even times that poet needs to muse on those three topics but should shroud them in burlap or bellow of them in a whisper or sketch them beneath a larger radiantly colorful painting with them only peeking out between the grooves.

Whatever way they are spoken, it should not so visibly methodical. With Solomon's poetry, the audience could anticipate the verses from a classic love song remixed by the newest "neo-soul" singer. When he spoke of artists whose time was too short lived, he would mention Donny

Hathaway, but could not name a song. He would speak on love with mention of Roberta Flack knowing his only association with her was through Lauryn Hill. His racism was limited to the Malcolm and Martin, Rosa and Harriet, slavery and Jim Crow and only in their most textbook descriptions. Now Solomon as host was wonderful, he could invigorate the crowd to its feet, make the most nervous speaker feel like an orator, and at times his poetry was inspiring; and, because he was so charismatic, no matter how hollow the words, how expected the phrases, how stale the imagery, it always came across as charming.

"Thanks for being so concerned Solomon, but I don't plan to stop again. I didn't pick the last break. You know how it is; things got a bit hectic that's all. So, what new poets have swept the audience away since I left?"

"You remember the last time you were here, the sista I saw you talking to. Ummmm dag, what was her name?"

Kyle feigned forgetfulness and then said, "Yakini, I think."

"I see she left a big impression on you. That isn't a name that is easily remembered, unless you have taken time to think on it."

Kyle pretended not to hear the comment at the end of the statement, but Solomon could see the smile Kyle tried quickly to tuck into the corners of his mouth.

"She's the new mental motivator, huh?"

"Seems that way, the crowd loves her, but she is still too shy to look at the audience for long, and she still lugs that notebook with her. I don't even think she reads from it, but that book is her blankie, keeps her safe on stage."

"Does she come every week?"

Kyle was hoping that tonight would happen to be the night that he would run into her again. For weeks after their conversation, he wished he'd asked for her number. He thought several times about coming to Harmony just to try to bump accidentally into her. But with his new position, he had no time for socializing. Odd that he was a poet, a writer, and it was his writing that had opened the door to being a professor, and it was being a professor that took away his writing. Took away his time to sit and think and wonder and compose and erase and type and read and type and think and wonder and think and look and observe and compose and erase.

Yeah, it was odd that his success in writing had taken away his ability to do it. That is the life of a writer, writing is wonderful cathartic inspiring beautiful and doesn't pay a penny—especially poetry. So, when his collection became critically successful (it was a sad reality that although he was well known by professors, thinkers, and poetry lovers he never made enough to pay his bills through his life's collection of emotions, beliefs, and thoughts) the university called, he took the position thinking he would be able to pay bills and still have time for his writing. Setting your own hours sounds like a dream, but there are no hours in education. There is always research to do, books to read, lectures to compose, papers to read and eventually your career becomes your life.

"She hasn't missed a night yet."

But before Solomon could finish his answer, Kyle saw her walk in and tried to keep his face focused on Solomon, but Solomon saw the quick redirection of his eyes and looked back to see the cause.

"There she is, but—I guess you knew that already," he grinned at Kyle.

Kyle lowered his eyes and let that smile rise like the sun the same way he did the night he talked to her. She was as beautiful as he had remembered. Her hair was pulled back with a scarf with a large afro protruding from behind. The ginger-colored shirt that touched her skin allowed him to see the orange undertones of her complexion. The chocolaty burnished lipstick allowed him to close in on her beautiful smile. Her teeth weren't perfect; she had a slight overbite. But it fit her. Her face was like sculpted copper and looked to be both incredibly soft and strongly angular at the same time. Kyle took in each blink of her eyelids, the pursing of her lips as she spoke to her friend, the sway of her hips as she balanced herself on the stiletto boots she wore, he took it all in, and smiled just as she noticed him at the bar.

He could tell that she saw him. Although she didn't make any gesture to acknowledge his smile, she didn't wave or nod her head, she didn't do the fake smile back, or even mouth "hello." She just looked at him, and in her eyes, he saw a vague sense of remembrance from across the room. He knew he wouldn't make the same mistake. He would not walk out of Harmony tonight not knowing if he would ever see her again. He would speak to her, exchanged numbers, and make some real connection so on their next encounter her remembrance would instead be a reflection on a wonderful experience.

The walk over to her table seemed to be incredibly long. Harmony was a small intimate setting and his walk could've been no more than a mere ten steps away, but the random thoughts that clouded his mind as he journeyed over made it seem much longer.

"Hello Yakini. How've you been?"

Now she instantly knew exactly who Kyle was when he came over, truthfully, she had noticed him as soon she entered the club, but she had played it off. And as he talked to her now she let the game continue. She looked at him distantly, with a puzzled look on her face. She didn't want to seem to be over zealous over a simple recollection of her name.

"Sorry, but um have we met before?"

He smiled. "Yes we have. However, it has been a while."

That smile was just as she had remembered, and it seemed to cause her to lose her position in the game.

"Hello Kyle. It's nice to see you again. It's definitely been a while."

He got the joke and smiled. Her style was what drew him to her. He liked the fact that she wasn't overly exerting herself to get his attention. He liked the way that she was confident and poised and didn't emit waves of desperation. Not to say that she should in any way be desperate, but sadly so many women have bought into the theory of the pending extinction of the black man and the scarcity of good black men, that they are truly becoming too eager. But not this sista, she was assertive, not aggressive. She made eye contact, carried on great conversation with a touch of sarcasm and dry-humor that confirmed her intelligence and genuine sense of humor.

"Did you come to grace us with a bit of your poetic genius tonight?" She smiled, a sweet smile, one that was as smooth as caramel on a hot summer day as she waited for his response.

"No, I only came as an onlooker tonight. I was hoping to find a little inspiration. I haven't written in a long time. Do you mind if I join you and your friend? I came alone tonight."

"No, I don't mind at all. You don't mind either, right Naomi?"

Pretending to be overly engrossed in the band and her drink, as if she hadn't been listening to the entire conversation, Naomi looked up at Kyle and said, "Oh hi, didn't see you there. What did you ask Yakini?"

Yakini shook her head and answered for her friend, "She doesn't mind."

The night was going well, the poetry was nice, the music was soothing, and the company was pleasurable. Not many words were said at the table, but the unspoken conversation was nice. The body language told stories that the mouths would have never uttered, the smiles confirmed that they each were hearing the same things, and a few times, they both closed their eyes and seemed to be speaking to one another in some other dimension. Yeah, the company was definitely pleasurable. Just as Yakini was absorbing this feeling, allowing it to permeate her thoughts, she faintly heard her name being called.

The stage was no longer a place of fear for Yakini, although she still got butterflies and her hands shook a little when she held her papers. The difference now was that her voice was clear, her eyes scanned the room, and she looked forward to her name being called. Tonight, she had prepared a piece; she had practiced it most of the week, but since Kyle was here she could finally do the one that she wrote that first night they met. After their first encounter, she went home and wrote, picturing Kyle not only to be a man that had piqued her interest, but had been the one sent for her.

It is odd that she wrote it considering she was not one to fall quickly for a guy no matter how attractive. She'd been carrying this piece in her bag each week hoping he would come back and she could read it and watch his expression.

3 EXHIBITIONISM

I thought I was ready to do this piece, I thought I really was ready to get up here and read this one, but as soon as I hold it in my hand I feel like this is my first time on the stage and I can't bear to look up cause if I do then I might actually make eye contact with him, and he may somehow figure out that this is for him, and if he did I would be so embarrassed. I barely know him, hell I don't know him. Well I know his name and what he does. I think he's a teacher or something. Ok well it is time to say something, how long have I been up here already.

"Good evening Harmony. This piece is somewhat new, well actually not new, I wrote it a few months back but never read it, and I figured tonight was as good a night as any to try it out. So here goes. It is called "His Words"

Peace is written on his face, etched into the ebony
creases of his smile lines
It is written within the curve of his lips –
Hidden behind his eyelids when he closes them to smile
Peace is written on his lips as they move so swiftly
As if eager to let the words slip from them and land on
my ears
Sound waves that wash over my thoughts ease my fears

After rushing, his tongue pushing out each syllable as if rendering a Gift for me in each syllabic utterance
And when it falls onto my ears I am cleansed
His words seep in and rush out to meet my awaiting orifices
In curvaceous rises and falls I pause
Close my eyes enjoying the feel of his words on my mind

Peace engages and I simply breathe deep
His smell filling my head although I have never smelled him
Nor do I know the name of his scent
I inhale this aroma into my long-term memory
So when he is gone I can close my eyes,
Meditate, and draw him in to me daily
And his essence can pour over me and I can
Be drenched in his aromatic scent and I can
Feel Inspired by his peace all over again

I take every word in and eat them as if they
Are delicacies prepared for me
Made for me, created small, bite size as if to be nibbled
And their flavor was created just for me to
Take and place on my tongue and allow them
To simply fade into my being
His words to me melt as mints and chocolates
Sweet and distinct and divine
His peace ingested into my being and I long to see his peace on his face

I long to hear the words flow from his beautiful lips and fall onto my thoughts
So I simply
Close my eyes and breathe deep and allow his aromatic scent
Again to seep deep deep into me
And I smile his peace on my face.

4 REUNION

"Very nice piece."

He is smiling, and I know that he knows that the poem was for him, but neither of us says a word more on the poem. We simply listen to the others come to the mic and take us away to distant lands while we sit in our chairs and our minds open wide as the open space, and we drink and smile and laugh and say "ugh" and "ah" and "uh uh uh" at their words and stories.

When we part, I take out a card. It is one of my old business cards. I simply cross out the number and write my home number down, and we exchange cards. He takes notice of the card and looks up at me as if he has a question, then he shakes his head.

"I don't work there anymore. Why that look?"

"I just remembered some things that I read in this magazine, and I was wondering if the words were yours. I used to buy it a lot."

"I know."

It had only been a few months. A few short months since she walked away from what her mother and friends all told her was a once in a lifetime opportunity. People use that phrase so loosely that it doesn't mean anything at all anymore. Once in a lifetime, was that to say that she should forever be bound to a job that neither challenged nor satisfied her anymore? She had sat and contemplated how she would survive after leaving, wondered if she would be able to live, financially, at the level at which she had become accustomed to living. It took her months to save enough money to keep her from needing another nine for five for at least a year, so she could just write for herself with no one else to give her direction or deadlines. It took months to decide on an action that would take only minutes, minutes to compose one short unrefined resignation letter, a vague note that gave no solid reason to Jacquelyn Jordan – Ms. Jordan, who was the person who had guided Yakini's fate for the past seven years.

Seven years of writing, constant writing. In the start, it was a dream come true, a job where she simply was allowed to write and be creative, but then the magazine became more commercial. The articles that had once pushed her to think, consider alternative possibilities, go against conventionalism, now had to be politically correct, had to be wide ranging (had to appeal to the masses, the majority, and ignore the very audience its initially tried to give voice to). Yakini had been with the magazine from its conception, before the commencement, in the foreplay of its conception when Ms. Jordan was merely Jackie, and she and Yakini sat and talked over how wonderful and innovative a media company for brown and black young women would be. Not the Essence, Ebony, and Vibe generation, but the one that followed. It was for the one that wanted Vogue, Elle, and Mademoiselle, but also wanted Bossip and Shaderoom. This was a new woman of color, who was chic, but still a little ghetto. Ghetto, not in the negative hood rat, ignorant, Hollywood version of the word, not the offensive denotation of the word, but rather the loving realistic side of the word, ghetto as in the real sister from the block who indeed had "overcome," but had not completely assimilated. The sister, who was educated and classy, but also was the one who on the way to her corporate America job blasted old school Tupac and Biggie in her luxury sedan. The company was to incorporate Gucci and Prada with Bagwell, Brandon Blackwood, and Telfar, mixing Miles Davis and Angela Davis, informing this new sister on issues from financial investments to romantic rendezvous, inspiring sisters to the levels of the Giovanni and Morrison. It was a vision, a mission. But that was years ago when Ms. Jordan was Jackie, and Yakini was naïve. In this intimate conversation, they mulled over how needed this publication was, but here it was seven years later and Yakini left her letter on Jackie's large mahogany desk in her large ivory painted office with plush eggplant carpet and walked silently out.

Yakini took with her only what would fit in the plastic crate she kept under her desk. She left the plaques hanging, the awards sitting on the shelf in all their phony glory. She left them all. She took her books, her pens, and her pictures. Armed with all she needed to go home and write for herself; she pushed open the large glass doors and walked to the parking deck. She smiled as she walked away.

She would miss Jackie; she would miss the new girls, whom she had begun to preen. She would miss the interviewing of some of the most fabulous people in the music and fashion industry. However, she would not miss writing lies, she would not miss omitting the articles that were too ethnic as, Ms. Jordan now called them, and mostly she would not miss what La Chic Noire had become.

Kyle now remembered why the name had been so easy to remember, other than its being connected to this beautiful woman. It had been on the byline of an article on the poetry night at Harmony.

He had never connected the two. The article was written months before he noticed her at Harmony. It was an okay article, mentioned some of the well-known poets who had come for special shows at Harmony in the past, praised the food and ambiance, but when he had read the piece, it lacked realism. It seemed to be an objective listing of facts, instead of a personal narrative of an inviting social experience at what he knew was one of the most welcoming, homey, comforting places in town. He wondered why she had written it in that way. He knew she loved it here. It was written on her face when she had gotten on stage. She spoke to the staff on a first name basis now and was known by most of the other poets on the register.

"Now I remember, you wrote the piece on Harmony, right?"

She was little embarrassed. "Yes, along time ago. I actually wrote it before I came to any of the readings here. I needed one more place to cover in the entertainment section and a friend told me this was one of the hot spots in town. I called the club and got a few details, but now that I've become 'Harmonized', I wish I'd come here before writing it. The article certainly didn't do this place justice at all."

"It was a nice piece, but I did think it lacked a certain personal touch to it."

He was being honest, and it was refreshing. So often, men try to be overly nice—saying anything to impress and caress the ego of the woman that they are either courting or hoping to court. If they truly understood women though, then they would simply just be themselves. It takes entirely too much time to pretend to be someone you're not only to then try to slowly reveal yourself piece by piece. Dating is not a strip tease and in the case of being yourself you should simply stand butt naked in front of the other and allow them to take it all in the good, bad, ugly, funny, sad, pitiful, and gorgeous parts of your personality in all its exposed glory.

"Thanks for being candid about the piece. I'm glad you didn't try to make it sound like I'd written some spectacular, in depth, heart-felt, article.

Honesty is hard to come by, especially in the arts where far too many writers, painters, photographers, and musicians don't say how a work makes them feel, but BS and hide behind the façade of simply having an open-mind. But most of the time open-mind is a pseudonym for phony."

He smiled at how in depth al her answers were but at the same time he enjoyed having a real conversation with a woman he found to be as attractive as she was intelligent, "Yeah, a lot of time people claim to have this vast open-mind. But that phrase implies a use of the mind, and saying you like something when you don't isn't being open-minded. It isn't being artistic. It isn't being real. It is simply being polite, which can be okay."

"True, but at times it can be more harmful and hurtful to the person than simply being honest and allowing the person that you're being honest with to get a real opinion. Criticism can inspire movement, growth, evolution, and change. Your being polite would be comparable to me asking an appraiser to look at my home only to have him tell me it is worth ten times its worth–it sounds nice, but at closing does me no good. Hell, I'm happy you told me that, and I hope that even if it is something new I've written that you'll be just as open and honest so that I can continue to better myself."

The conversation went by like a good tennis match with each player sending a hard blow of opinion to the other to volley off of only to play it just right with a comment of his or her own. They both were on the same page on honesty at least and they knew that it is hard to come by and when you do it is like sitting in the sunshine in mid-May when you know that winter is truly gone and summer is still far enough off for the heat to be bearable.

Some girls are turned on by nice shoes, an immaculately dressed man, or even a few compliments, but for Yakini intelligence and honesty were some powerful aphrodisiacs. She could feel the smile rushing to her cheeks and pouring out of her eyes as she basked in this small glimmer of honesty and he took notice and smiled back.

"Well, Mr. Niane, I hate to leave so abruptly, but I

promised my girl I'd 0meet her later for drinks. Maybe we can continue this conversation another time?"

"That is a definite possibility."

He had a very nice smile; she noticed again and this one was even nicer because he kind of blushed behind the smile until he actually looked away. It was adorable.

5 ANSWERING MACHINES

Inversions

Odd that the pursued or the seemed initial prey
Has now taken on the mission of seeking out predators
Unknown to me when this role reversal began
The moment when man figure he no longer needed to pursue
And no longer actively engages in the pursuit but only has to wait
To sit stoically and patiently bait his prey to come and sit on his lap
The confusion does not merely end with the player's new positions
But continues with the use of flamboyant arrays of physical Displays
By the prey to be seen Instead of stealthy camouflage, secretive
Smiles, nods and glances
The prey now enhances its chances of being caught, bagged, and hung out
to dry
Batting eyes, flashing teeth,

And when all else fails
The prey simply lies down and waits

Yakini was on time, but it appeared her girl, Triesha, was late. Triesha was one of the younger girls that had started writing for LCN before the Yakini's exit. Tri was a sweetie; at times, it was her downfall. She loved quick and hard and often, which made for many nights of passion and romance, but even more nights of tears and sobs. Most of the men she dated took her niceness as a weakness instead of seeing it as a gift that can be used as nourishment for their own strength and hers if they could only use it correctly.

Tonight was going to be another night of Tri's deciding if she would stay with Quincy or not. They had been going out for nearly a year, and he had given no solid reason for a breakup, if lack of quality time wasn't counted. That was his problem—time. He had plenty of it, but it wasn't for Tri. It was for his many jobs, responsibilities, and duties to his ex-wife, children, parents, friends, and any other entity that could find a way to his list of priorities. These pop-ups were placed on this list behind the constants— money and his kids—and in front of his woman. The odd thing is that often, black men are looked at negatively for being uninvolved with their children, especially if they are no longer with the mother, and for being unmotivated and this brother was the polar opposite of all these negative stereotypes.

Triesha loved him for these things, but hated their presence at times too, because these two wonderful qualities had somehow melded together into a mass that wedged a wall between them.

"Hey girl, have you been waiting on me a long time?"

"Nah, just got here a little while ago. I went to Harmony first. How's Quincy?"

"Girl same old same old tired story, his jobs are endless, his ex is needy, and his family is dependent, but otherwise he is the same wonderful man, well he was when I saw him two weeks ago."

"Two weeks? Why such a long break? You two giving things a rest for a while?"

"No, this is normal for us. We spend more time making phone calls, sending text messages, and writing emails, than we ever spend together. Not that I don't love that man, I promise I do. It's just hard for me to think he really cares when he doesn't make time for me girl. It's wearing on my Spirit, and I am tired of wondering what if he's cheating or if I were thinner would he make more time, or if I did this or that. It is beginning to. . ."

"Tri, stop girl. I know you are not letting a brother, not even a good brother like Quincy, start you to doubting yourself, girl. Now I've known you for a while now, and you may be naïve in some ways, a little too nice for my taste, but you've never been insecure. Your niceness was never a runoff of insecurity issues. Did he say something to you?"

"No, he says he loves me as is. I talk to him constantly even if I don't see him, so I know there isn't another woman."

Yakini looked away not wanting her doubt of Quincy's fidelity to cloud Tri's decision.

Triesha saw Yakini divert her eyes, but didn't want to argue, she had had to fight this battle of her man's honesty too many time with her mother and friends to face it with Kini tonight, "Anyways, it just hurts to think he can go two sometimes three weeks without seeing me as if I'm just a marginal part of his life, a perk to be played with only when there is extra time."

"Have you thought about getting out of it? I mean if it's bringing you down to a point of second guessing your own worth, then maybe it is time to walk."

"Of course I've thought about it, but then I am like it isn't his issue—it's mine. I mean, am I really so needy that I have to have him feed my ego? Do I have to have him constantly wanting to be in my presence for me to know that my presence is worth being in? I don't know. Girl, all I know is that I love that man and I don't want to leave him. I just want more time. I don't want to throw out a good man because we have some time issues."

"I feel you, but I just think maybe you need to be alone."

"I've been alone sweetie, I was alone before I met him and well this is better that what I had before at least. And Kini not to be mean, but all this time I've known you I've never seen you in a serious relationship. I mean yeah you date but what about you Kini, who's strumming your strings now?"

She hadn't thought about her being alone in a long time. It just was. It was like her having brown eyes or wide hips, she knew they were there but she didn't dwell on it.

"Girl, strumming my strings? I don't have a real player. I mean I have someone to come and tighten 'em up when they need it."

The truth was that no notes had rose from those cords in a while. Hell in all honesty, Kini didn't even know if they still played.

They both laughed, but deep down Yakini began to think on her singleness and counted the months it had been since she had so much as had a date. It had definitely been a while. She remembered the card in her pocket from Kyle. She put her hand in her pocket and felt the embossments —the small ridges smooth yet firm under her fingertips. Maybe she would call him even though that was going against the norm. But hell, the norm obviously had not worked, so time for something new.

Three rounds of Cosmos into the night, Yakini thought it might be her time to leave. She motioned for her check and asked the bar tender to call her a cab.

"You're getting ready to go so soon Kini? Quincy is stopping by here; I thought maybe the three of us could hang out a little longer."

"Sweetie, you said it's been two weeks. The last thing the two of you need is a third party to impede on the rush you're gonna make to get out of this bar."

~~~~~~~~~~~~~~

"You've reached Kyle Niane. I'm not in at the present time. Leave me your name, number, and a brief detailed message, and I'll return your call as soon as possible."

She hadn't thought about his not answering and the awkward first conversation with the answering machine. She hadn't thought that she'd have to get it right the first time, no nervous laughter, no trivial banter, just jump right in after the tone and actually say something simple, yet intelligent, and hope that her voice was not slurring after three Cosmos.

Beeeeeeeep.

"Hi Kyle, this is Yakin from Harmony. I just thought I would give you a call, um" she lost her train of thought. "There's ah no particular message. Simply wanted to say hi."

She pressed the pound key and then 2. Listening to the message, she didn't think she wanted to keep that one. She pressed 3 to erase and re-record. After the third or fourth try, she was satisfied that the mix of sexy, cool confidence and nonchalance was just the right blend.

Yakini went to sleep that night and slept deep. No dreams fluttered on her pillow to announce the pending dawn. The sun poured into the creases in her eyes the minute they began to part. That bartender must've been a newbie; he didn't water any of the drinks down last night. She noticed the notification for a voicemail on her phone.

"Was that there last night?" She shook her head in an attempt to remember but nothing came. She picked up the receiver and typed in her code.

"Hey Yakini this is Kyle. I was just giving you a call hoping we could meet up for drinks. But as the phone was ringing I remembered that you went out with your girl. So, it's a little before eleven; give me a call when you get this."

She hadn't even noticed the message before going to bed last night, but then again, she didn't notice much when she
~~~~~~~~~~~~~~

got home last night. A bit flustered, she could feel the rush of blood to her cheeks, which hadn't happened in years. Pressing play again, she listened to the rise and fall of his voice; it was soothing and creamy. She looked at the clock and saw that it was too early to call him, maybe after a few cups of coffee. Strong and dark with just a splash of cream and a little chocolate added for sweetness. Walking to the couch with coffee and half a bagel, looking at the phone made her smile.

~~~~~~~~~~~~~

Not much is on the television today, being a Saturday afternoon. Slowly flipping the channels looking for a few minutes at a movie that seemed familiar and finding the usual teen flicks and eighties movies, I decide today is instead a day for a warm bath and a good book. So I grab my new copy of Toni's *Love*, which I'm looking forward to almost as much as the pending relaxation that waits on me in the bath with steam made heavy with of lavender oil, aromatic and luscious, not to mention the bubbles, which are a nice added touch. And just as I turn the fifth page, trying to get a feel for the novel, I hear the phone ringing. Normally I would let voicemail take the call while I enjoyed my time soaking away the week. But not today.

Feet, soapy and wet, touch the hardwood floor of the bedroom, a moment late. Damn, the ringing stopped. I quickly dial the number back.

"Hello."

"I was just about to leave a message. How are you today?"

Smiling and walking back to the bath the, with the cordless to my ear, I step in slowly, as to not make a loud splash.

"I'm good; I got your message last night. Well actually, this morning. I guess I didn't notice the notification."

"Yeah, I got yours this morning too. I was pleasantly
~~~~~~~~~~~~~

surprised to hear your voice coming from my voicemail. Guess we had our wires crossed, huh?"

The line was trite, but cute so I laugh and he does too. Cliché. Yeah it was, but that's ok.

"What are your plans for the afternoon?"

"I was thinking of curling up with a good book. I just started one of my Morrison novels I've had forever that I haven't read yet. Other than that, I don't really have any set plans."

"Hmm, ok. Would you like to join me today?"

"Where are we going?"

"We? So that's a yes."

"I guess it is. What are your plans for us?"

"Actually, I don't' have a set agenda. I thought that between the two of us we'd come up with something."

"I'm sure we can. What time?"

"How about I come over in an hour to get you?"

Directions were given and receivers were placed to cradles. Laying back for a moment and closing my eyes, I thought about what to wear. Simple denim jeans and a denim blazer. White tee shirt with the word "Humanity" written across it in black, black boots, and hair loose today and straightened.

The doorbell rang. He was fifteen minutes early.

"Hi."

"Hi, come in."

He walked in.

6 ECLECTICS

Jordache Love
Jordache stone washes
High top converse
High top fades
High right low left
When rap was positive
And Michael was black
Passing notes in math
Do you love me?
Check yes or no
Simple love
No games
No playas
Hot summers
Community pools
Marco polo love
Simple love

Where there were no games
And no players

Her home was warm and inviting. The smell of lavender was in the air. A book lay open on the sofa. A half full cup of coffee sat on top of the mahogany slab of wood that sat atop a mahogany elephant as a base. The sofa was red. There were lush chocolate pillows sprawled against its wide

back. The chairs in the room were all different. There was a 60's inspired lounge chair and a contemporary straight back chaise. The floors were hardwood and shiny. A tall lamp stood in the far corner with an oriental shade. The art was all black and from different periods some African some African American from the renaissance to modern sketches, but none of it seemed to be forced. The area rug lay under the sofa and chairs and was full of asymmetrical shapes in reds, blues, and yellows on a tan background. The colors filled his head in a matter of seconds. On a small table near a bay window in the other room, a bouquet of lilies in an assortment of colors emerged from a clear vase. The table it sat on was made of stone, not marble, but a black shiny stone with etchings of white and gray. He looked at her. She was watching his eyes dance around the room. There was a smile on her face. She had on a simple outfit, which was good. He was glad she hadn't gone overboard and dressed as if they were going on a late-night dinner date. He had known women who would have put on four-inch heels or some other impracticable piece of clothing, which was put on not for comfort sake but to show off some part of their body that they wanted to draw attention to only to get annoyed when he actually gave attention to it.

They walked out of the door to his car. It was a nice car—stock wheels nothing fancy. She was happy that he had not gone overboard with chrome, rims, and over-the-top and flashiness. He opened the door and she got in.

The sun had warmed the leather seats just enough that it was comfortable and homey when she sat down. She reached over and opened his door for him extending to him the same courtesy he had given to her. The engine turned over quietly and soon the sound of Stevie was swooning in her ears.

The ride was as smooth as the sound of "My Cherie

Amour" in her ears, and she closed her eyes for a moment and inhaled again.

~~~~~~~~~~~~~~

The park was nice today with a sky that was a tranquil blue and crystal clear, and the air hung with the smell of freshly cut green grass. They sipped wine and talked for hours on every subject imaginable from literature to the electric slide and its occult like charm that called way too many overage dancers to venture onto dance floors after one too many mixed drinks. They both laughed when telling stories of their own up-in-age relative who had embarrassed him or herself at the last wedding reception after that song was played and they wanted to show that they "still had it." They talked about nearly everything, nearly but not all.

Although he knew that she worked at a magazine he read at one time, he had no idea of what she was doing now. And she knew that he was a teacher of sorts, but no idea what subject or what school, or what level even for that matter. They both assumed that the other was single, but neither outwardly asked. There was no ring line, that visible sun-line where rings leave their territory markings, on his hand. And she had actually given him the correct number and address and allowed him to come inside, so he assumed that those were signs of liberty from attachment. As the sun began to set, they realized they had been at the park for hours now, but neither was truly ready to call it quits. But the grumble of stomachs full of butterflies and merlot and not much else began to tell them it was time at least to relocate to a scene with food.

"Want to grab a bite to eat on the way back?" She said it casually.

He caught the hint. Back to where... her place his place, he wasn't sure. The implication made it seem that their destination was to be the same, so he smiled that smile that caught her eye the very first night they met with eyes
~~~~~~~~~~~~~~

diverting, closing, and then shining with anticipation.

"There's a Thai restaurant on Lennox Boulevard that I've wanted to try for a while. You like spicy food?"

At the restaurant, the maître d' asked if they would be eating in; she said yes, and he smiled that smile again. At the table, he ordered more wine, a sweet Riesling to offset the spicy foods to come. She thought it an odd combination, the sweet and hot, but the juxtaposition of tastes was pleasant.

"So we have sat and talked nearly all evening, but I haven't gotten much personal info on you."

"You haven't asked anything. . ."

"Well I think that goes both ways."

"Well I guess, I'm asking now," He mimicked her sarcasm.

"Let's see, I am an only child. I have a daughter who is ten, Nia Jordan, who talks more like she's 40. She is with her grandparents for a little while. What else, I am in transition between my old career, and my new one. I have no pets, a few close friends, and I'm a Leo. I am a Christian, but choose not to be "religious" because I think it is hypocritical to found a church for someone who came to destroy the dogma that man had begun to construct around the physical structure of the church while slowly sucking the spirit out of it. I am single, never married, and I used to be a vegetarian."

He laughed at her as she spoke in her most professional voice. It was as if she were answering for a job interview.

"So that is the new condensed modern English version, huh? I would have preferred the annotated edition with small stories that give faces to all those facts."

Then he took her game and ran with it, "As for me, I am a Gemini, so you know that tomorrow I may not be this sweet, right? I am a professor at Northtown College, and I teach a course on African Diaspora Literature. I've been in Georgia now for about seven years. I relocated from Philly after being there for about two years, and before Philly it was Chicago, and before Chicago it was Nevada, and before Nevada there were lots of other places. I have three sisters and no brothers, and yes I was forced to wear heels, but only once and they were really cute with the pearls my older sister put on me. As for religion, I usually tend to stay off the subject, but since you brought it up, I am still searching."

"Ok so I got the brief edition too." She giggled at his ability to roll with her sense of humor and then through him for a loop, "But I see you didn't touch the single/separate/divorced/or married issue."

"Well I'm here, I've been here for over," he looked down at his watch unsure as to how long they had been together, "8 hours with you today, and my phone hasn't rung once."

"Separated or divorced?"

He looked at her as if he was annoyed then let a smile slip, "Divorced, seven years."

"That inspired the move?"

"No, the move inspired the divorce."

After the fried ice cream, they both decided that they had had enough to eat, more than enough in all actuality and decided it was time to go. The ride home was quicker than they both anticipated. At the door, she gave him a hug and a kiss on the cheek. His arms squeezed her waist closely to him, and she inhaled him in and held her breath to let the memory of his scent set in for her dreams to come later that night.

"Call me when you get in, just so I'll know you made it home safely."

As she closed the door and leaned back on it, with a smile on her face as wide as the grill of an old school Cadillac, 1972 Eldorado style with the huge chrome grill, she thought her cheeks might actually explode. As she took her shoes off and ran her bath water her phone rang, but tonight she heard it and picked it up, on the third ring—can't look too anxious.

"Watcha doin?" The comfort in his voice was nice. The

fact that he had slipped into his casual I'm talking from my soul and not being all uptight and professional word choices made her smile.

"Gettin' in the bath tub."

"Can I join you?"

"Ewww, I know you not trying to get fresh with me."

"Fresh, what other way is there to be with someone sooooooo finnnnne?"

They both giggled. People have forgotten how to flirt, joke, have fun and it felt good to just be silly.

"What are you doing?"

"Chillin' on the sofa watching some Law and Order: SVU."

"Oh really, what is the crime tonight?"

"This girl's body was discovered in the trunk of her brother's-in-law car. Right now, Briscoe's interrogating him, but you know he didn't do it. The first one they interview is never the one."

"Right. Well don't tell me anymore. I'll catch it in replay later tonight. I had a great time with you today."

"Great huh, not just good. You trying to make a brother blush over here, right?"

"No, I'm for real. Did you have a nice time?"

"Nice, nah. It was aaaa-ight. I mean it was ok."

They both laughed again, and she closed her eyes and enjoyed the feeling of being so comfortable. She couldn't remember the last time a man had made her laugh so often or so real. She had laughed on dates, polite laughs, or even laughs at the guy when he was in the bathroom, but for the first time in years she laughed and actually had fun with no pretension behind it.

"I guess I'm going to let you go so you can actually bathe, don't want you to just sit and soak. Scrub girl scrub. Get behind your ears, and get those elbows too."

"Whatever. Call me in the morning."

"So I make wake-up calls now."

"No, but since you have to go to work and all, you might

as well call me since you'll be awake."

"Oh yeah, so what do you do during the days now since you stopped the nine-to five grind?"

"Write. Sip coffee. Dust and fold clothes. Write some more and then take a nap."

"I wish. I remember when I did that before teaching. But anyways, I will most definitely call you in the morning."

"Goodnight Mr. Niane."

"Goodnight Miss. Truth."

She smiled, he smiled, and the screens both went black.

7 STREAM OF WORDS

African musk puffs dance in air
Floating in long thin gray streams
Jazzy smooth notes sing of love and lust
As the stick slowly falls to dust
Intoxicating aroma fills the room
While speakers continue to boom with bass
Of drums beating and silky vocals crooning
A hand in hair swirls twists fumbles through
The bushes grown upon my head
Fingers brush my neck
Tug short ropes formed at my nape
Lights dimmed
Candle's glow dance on walls in slow fluid movements
Beautiful onyx floating in a sea of ivory glances at me
As thin veils of mahogany slowly wedge between
Onyx and me and the ivory sea

The phone rang. Six thirty, didn't think he would call so early, but I need to get up. Today will be productive. I haven't written anything since I left LCN. Actually, there had been bits and pieces starts and middles of things written, but nothing had complete. I went from wanting to write poetry to writing a novel to thinking about doing freelance magazine articles, but had in actuality done next to nothing for the past few weeks.

She picked up the phone and put on her most Bond girl voice, "Good morning Kyle."

"Who?"

"Umm, hello."

He laughed in her ear, "Now what if I had been your real boyfriend calling this morning, what in the world would you have said?"

"I would have said. Good morning Kyle, but that would be months away from today I'm sure."

"Cute answer. It sounds like you're already wide awake."

"No, the ringing woke me."

"Well I'm on my way out the door, but I'm glad I called. Your voice is a nice way to start off my day."

"Yours too. Have a beautiful, wonderful, productive day, okay?"

"I'll try, but I'll settle for two out of three of those adjectives today."

The smell of coffee was in the air within minutes and my hair twisted in a bun with chop sticks perched top my head like a robin's nest— meticulously messy. The hum of the computer and the drip of the dark roast were the only sounds to be heard in the house. What in the world will I work on today? I have to concentrate on one thing and finish it. Searching for a file on the computer on which to focus, I settle on the one that I was writing for a freelance article. It's interesting, but not overly analytical. It doesn't need as much research as it does polishing and emotion. The sound of dripping is replaced with slow sips and messy slurps, the hum continues, and the click of keys adding to the melody this morning, along with a little Anthony Hamilton—man this brother sounds like Sam Cook. The minutes and then hours pass by fairly quickly, and soon I am actually reading a finished piece, a nice four-page article on the new trend in natural hair. It was from a first person point of view with a few quotes by friends, women I've bumped into while shopping, and a few beauticians, most of whom were not advocates for going 100% natural and many of whom actually added weaves, texturizers, and braid extensions as forms of the natural. The piece was objectives giving the pros and cons of going natural. I think I'll submit it to Hype Hair and maybe one or two others to see if I can get a bite from someone.

While I am looking through the files again, I find one adequately named "novel," which has been on this computer for two years now and has changed directions more times that my girl Camille's hair has changed colors over the years. It has been a romance novel, has been a metafictional piece, shoot it has even been a personal narrative, it has been a compilation of stories and poems that were to loosely form a novel, it has been a novel spinning in my mind that had warped from Pulitzer material to beach reading to soft erotica to a million other things. It has been.

Opening it and reading the first 20 pages, it seems that there are moments that this piece is truly wonderful. Writing has been a passion forever; it began in middle school as an escape from being the chunky smart girl and often the butt of many jokes. It became a best friend and this novel was my first attempt at a long work, I'd written poetry forever, short stories that had been published and many arenas, and more articles than I could count, but the novel was a dedication. It didn't take minutes, hours, or even months it took commitment and time, which I happen to have more of than ever before.

Before now I couldn't commit to one topic long enough to finish the novel. But more than topics, I couldn't commit to the characters for fear of being judged. The honesty it takes to write an article is marginal, poetry can be masked and the truth hidden, but prose in length caused her to be real with myself and to tear down the image I had taken years to construct for my parents, family, and friends. The personal narrative forced me to be honest and the more honest I became, the more I knew no one could ever be allowed to read it. But I'm stronger now... hell II was strong enough to leave LCN. Mama thought I was being selfish and foolish, *"You have a baby to think about girl... you can't be up there trying to find yourself now. You waited too long for all that. Just be happy being where you are sweetie. I think you've done great myself. Why can't you see that?"*

Even after hearing her comments, rather criticism wrapped in sweeties and honeys, and even having dad tell me over and over that I should reconsider, I walked.

I will finish this. I'm going to finish this thing. I know that it is in me to write this thing. I don't know what it is about, but I know that inside me I want to finish it. I need to call Jamison, hell I am sure she has put me on her list of has-beens. She was great at getting me into journals that I only dreamed of in college. If it had not been for her, I would have left LCN long ago. But, Jamison was my secret agent working to find stealthy avenues for me to express myself. Ghost writing on a few things and submissions under pseudonyms solicited with Jamison's help keep me sane for the last three years with Jackie. But, she gave up on this novel, too much time and too little proof. I am sure she will be shocked to hear me mention it again. But I need to write it, finish it, and even if it isn't an earth shattering new American novel, it will at least be complete. Unlike the articles, it is slowing coming along.

I take lines from chapters, pages from chapters, and some full chapters and transposed them into something new. Cutting and pasting the segments that seem most promising, I arrange them into a new blank document.

~~~~~~~~~~~~~~

The phone rang on page 50 or so, and she stopped.

"How is your day going?"

"Girl you know the novel, right?" She didn't have to say
~~~~~~~~~~~~~~

which novel or "the novel that I am writing" because anyone who knew her knew that she was working on "the novel."

"Yeah, how's it coming this time?"

"Started over on it today. "

"Hmph."

"Hmph what heifer?

"Girl this thing has been started over more times than your diets."

"Whatever. I am working on it, and I think I'm on a roll. I was just about to call Jamison and tell to get on the grind this time because I'm really

going to finish this time."

"So that is all that you're doing today? Want to go out tonight?"

"Girl while I have these weekends free I better take advantage of it. Nia'll be coming home soon."

"How is my Nelly-pooh?"

"Last time I talked to her, she loved it down there. Her grandma lets her do anything she wants."

"Ok well, wear something nice. The club has a strict dress code."

"Black dress it is."

"Again?"

Naomi knew Kini would wear black. That was all she wore out when they went out for a night on the town. Her self-image was so distorted that she couldn't see how beautiful she really was. She put up a great front.

Everyone thought she was confident and secure with the natural hair and the stilettos and jeans, but her girl knew that the jeans were worn because she was too ashamed to wear a short skirt and the heels were worn, even when they hurt, because Kini thought they made her legs look longer and maybe by a chance a little leaner. It hurt her that Kini was so insecure of her own beauty.

"Well I could wear my dark washed jeans with a cute

top."

"Heels, right?"

"You said there was a dress code, so yes heels."

"Well meet me tonight at my place around eight; it's free before ten and we need time for at least two or three drinks."

8 STEPPING SOLO

My Soul Cries

Eyes down cast toward floors
Smiling mask covers sores deep
Childhood games
Wounds ache of self-hate
Loathing the face daily reflected
Unattractive dark skin,
Wide nose,
Large lips,
Wide round hips,
Tears fall at home
Each carries her cross alone
Bearing America's lye
My soul cries
In every compliment –doubt
Inability to believe
Inside the self lies beauty
Only conceiving ugly imagery
Taunting names
The soul cries,
Eyes fall, glancing only at floors

Accepting America's mockery
Black girls forget their innate beauty
Search outside their skin
The secret lies within
Waiting to be retrieved,
Set free
Black girls are deceived
Pay self-worth as the cost
Heritage and self-love lost
Souls bought,
Enslaved,
Chained,
Physical changed
Blue contacts, blonde hair
Lies applied in styling chairs
Media displays assimilation as progress
Devastate self-acceptance
My soul cries

Yakini opted for the jeans with a cute black top. It was cut low in the front with bell sleeves and a fitted waist that hit right at her hips in a scrunched-up-I'm-not trying-too-hard- to-look-cute-messy rumple at the bottom. It had flecks of neon yellow in it that made it stand out. Her heels weren't too bad tonight. The heels were high and thin, but they were danceable. Her afro was picked out and the front was intricately corn rowed, her makeup was immaculate, but standing in the bathroom mirror all she saw were her hips, stomach, and the slight oncoming of what could be a second chin. At a size 16, the jeans fit perfectly, well tight but that is the point of that 2% Lycra in there right? Yakini didn't feel as sexy as she thought the outfit would make her feel.

A few glasses of wine lather she was on the way to Naomi's house and blasted the radio. Instead of Anthony tonight, it was Juvenile asking for slow motion. She felt good as she rode. She looked in the rear-view mirror often and saw that her face was really pretty, but it was never about her face. She rang the bell at five 'til eight; and of course, Naomi was not dressed.

"See, I knew you were gonna come here all cute and out dress me. You do it every time Kini."

This banter happened every night before they went out. Yakini half smiled and wished that she could just look smaller for one night, but she didn't dare mention it to Naomi, who had no idea what it felt like to be the fat girlfriend at the club.

In line at the club, Yakini fidgeted with her blouse pulling at the waist hoping that it wasn't showing her rolls around her stomach. She eyed the girls in line and a few of them saw her eyes and mistook her looks as flirting and gave back some of the most blazing "bitch don't look at me like that" looks to her. Yakini and Naomi walked in and walked over to order drinks first and take a seat to assess the crowd.

~~~~~~~~~~~~~

"Two Tequila Sunrises."

"$16.00."

The price of getting in the club has to be taken off so that a sister can at least buy a drink because brothers definitely don't do that anymore. Yakini thought of the night she ran into an "old friend" from college. They danced and had fun. When she went to the bar and ordered an expensive glass of wine, he asked the bartender for the same, but when the check came, he thought he was going to walk away and leave her to pay for both. He was out of his mind obviously to think that first he shouldn't have to buy her a drink and secondly to assume that she would pay for his. That was the end of their reunion, and they hadn't spoken since. The club was packed as usual with the five women to every man ratio that was expected in an Atlanta club. The music was nice and both women went out to dance.

Yakini told herself each night that they had left the club that she would not go back. That she would not go to a
~~~~~~~~~~~~~

place that made her feel so insecure and unappreciated, yet here she was on another night.

As soon as they neared the dance floor, a hand reached for Naomi and asked her to dance. She waved him off and walked on through the crowd. The boom of bass makes all hips sway in the club even those hips of Yakini that she feels so ashamed of at home. Here she dances with no inhibitions and has a blast for the first few minutes. Eventually her girl is persuaded to move on and dance with one or two guys.

The music continues and Yakini dances on, yet each passing song and the lack of prospects asking her to dance begin to weigh on her fun. But the music is fast and the beat allows her hips to make her mind forget to worry.

Just as she is dancing, the music begins to slow. R. Kelly begins to croon a steppers' jam, she feels the music slow her hips, and she dances on not wanting to stop completely and make herself noticed all alone on the dance floor. Eyes closed, as if she's in love with the music when in truth she does not want to open them because they will automatically look for someone to make contact with and when no one does she will feel alone on the floor, she dances, eyes closed, hips swaying, spirit slipping. After the song ends, she makes her way to the bar and orders another Tequila Sunrise. Naomi is gone for the night. She will periodically come over bringing some "nice" guy behind her to meet her "pretty" friend. They each smile politely, ask her name, and fain some excuse that liberates them from her presence. A pretty face—with size 16 hips.

She takes a sip of her drink; she looks up and sees Kyle. He is dancing close behind a pretty girl with long wavy hair; she looks Hispanic. His hands sit on her size 6 hips and he dances closely, follows her rhythm and beat. Yakini thinks about going to say hello, but her hips hold her back. She takes sip after sip. There are empty chaises on the side of the dance floor, and she goes to sit down. She sits and drinks and watches the dance floor.

She no longer can see Kyle and decides to finish off this

drink and order another. As she leans back her head to finish off her drink, she feels a hand on her shoulder.

"What are you doing here?"

Kini attempts to answer as if she had no idea Kyle was here tonight, "Hey… did expect to see you out here. I'm just hanging out with my girl. She's out there somewhere. What about you?" She doesn't mention the Hispanic girl. It's a club and people come to dance. He'd just think she was being over reactive anyways no need in starting that up tonight.

"It's my friend's birthday. The rest of my boys are back there."

He points over to the VIP section with balloons in black and silver all over.

"You having fun?"

She lies, smiles, and says she is having a great time.

"Your eyes don't say fun. They say something… but I'm not reading fun in there."

She looked away. Not pity. Please not pity. Like me, smile at me, laugh with me, hell laugh at me, but not pity. Don't pity the big girl sitting in the chaise drinking excessively because it's better than sitting with her purse in her lap doing nothing.

"You want to leave?"

She thought about it. Leaving was good. She didn't honestly want to be at the club. It was a good idea at first. The thought of going out dancing and having fun, but then reality set in and she was sitting alone again feeling fat and frustrated. Then she thought about his motives. Did he really want to leave, was he feeling sorry for her, or did he see an easy lay for the night?

"Yakini, I said do you want to leave? I'll go let my boy know and he can ride with someone else. Where's your girl?"

"I can send her a text."

She was leaving. She was going to go with him. He wasn't some guy she had met at a club and was going "home" with. She knew Kyle, liked him, and he must like her too, right?

"Walk with me over here to tell my boys."

As she walked over, there was a mixture of feelings. Initially she felt pretty, wanted, and slightly sexy, but the closer they got to the collection of men in VIP the more unsure she felt. Her thighs seem to be heavier than ever, her face felt shiny and sweaty, she looked down as he introduced her slightly glancing up to smile as he said her name to his friend. She saw that his friend had a look of awareness at the name, as if it had been mentioned before tonight. She shook his friend Simeon's hand, and they left together.

He put his hand on her elbow and guided her out of the club. The air felt good outside as they walked to his car. She could feel him looking at her, and for the first time she felt self-conscious in his presence.

His beauty made her feel inadequate, and that made her feel ashamed, ashamed more at her inability to love herself than her thighs or her rolls. Ashamed that if he knew how much she truly hated her body that he too would begin to see her inadequacies. She looked away as they walked in silence. He opened the door; she got in.

9 TRUTH SERUM

She reached over and unlocked his door for him. That was a thing she learned from watching her parents, how to be considerate of your mate. Her father had always unlocked her mother's door first and as he walked around, she would lean over and unlock his door. A simple affectionate act.

"So what is wrong Yakini? You look a little sad tonight. Every time I've seen you, you've looked happy and strong and radiant and tonight at the club when I saw you, I had to look twice 'because your eyes didn't look like the woman I knew. So what is it?"

"Nothing." A simple one-word answer.

"Whoa, I have a writer with nothing to say. Now I now it has to be something."

"Kyle, look it isn't really anything. I just wasn't really feeling the club scene."

"That's all?"

"Yeah."

"Yakini look, I know you don't know me that well, but I know that isn't all. Your face is still all closed in like you're holding in something that wants to come out."

"Kyle, why did you want to meet me initially? Was it only my words or what else was it?"

He squinted his eyes like the sunlight had just hit a mirror, and he was dazed momentarily.

"Umm, you. Your words, your presence, your beauty, just you. When your name was called, and I looked back and saw you getting your papers together I took notice. Then I watched you walk with so much confidence. Long strides and swaying hips had me hypnotized. Then you spoke and your voice was so sweet and clear and distinct. Then your words were as beautiful as your eyes, and I knew I had to meet you."

A tear rolled down her cheek, and she smiled. He saw it as she tried to wipe it quickly away with her fingers, and he wanted to know why she cried, but he knew she wasn't ready to say, so he didn't ask again.

"So you want me to take you back home tonight?"

"Um, where else can I stay?"

"With me. Well in my guest room that is."

"Guest room huh. I bet."

"What you thought you were going to come home and take advantage of me tonight… oh no girl. I'm not having any of that."

He smiled at her with a smile that said whatever is wrong; forget about it—for now at least. He pulled up to a quaint house near the campus where he taught. The porch light was on and shined on the red door. He came, opened her door, and took her hand to help her from the car. On the inside, the walls were the color of sand and the sofas, tan brown leather. She sat down and felt the softness that proved he lived in his house and didn't just stay in it. He brought her a cup of tea sweetened with honey and sat on the floor next to her feet with his back leaned up against her shins. She put her cup down and played in his hair and thought about how good it felt to just be here with him with no intention and no plans.

"So you want to tell me what was wrong earlier?"

10 EARLY RISERS

Softly knocking patiently waiting allowing you to casually stroll
Take your time peer through the peep hole ask who is knocking
Softly knocking patiently waiting allowing you to casually
Chains locks deadbolts alarms bells sirens screen the entrance of your heart
Softly knocking patiently waiting allowing you casual
Fingers slowly unlatching hands cautiously turning pressure slowly easing
Softly knocking patiently waiting allowing you
Feel the door cracking hear the hinges squeaking feel the knob trembling
Softly knocking patiently waiting allowing always knowing
Hear you fumbling turning pulling easing a gap in the wall between us
Softly knocking patiently waiting always knowing your desire
Hear your breathing increasing sound of your heartbeat racing
Softly knocking patiently always knowing your desire to have
Take your time unlock each lock peer through the peep hole

acknowledge
Softly knocking patiently knowing your desire to have open
Take your time ease the door slowly open acknowledge my presence
Softly knocking knowing your desire to have open doors
Take your time door slightly open acknowledging presence of my heart
Softly knowing your desire to have open doors of love
Take your time step away from the door acknowledge loves presence in my heart
Softly knowing your desire of open doors of loving connections
Take your time step away from the door acknowledge loves presence allow my presence
Softly your desire opens doors of loving connections between us
Step away from the door allow my presence to love your essence and softly open your desire

Yakini with her closed eyes feels his hair on her hand when he moves. He sits up and looks at her face. The night was not in his plans. He had no intentions to romance or to try and seduce her, not last night at least. But he had to be honest, he had thought rather extensively about how he would eventually romance and seduce her. He had thought about it the first night he met. He had thought about it each time they had seen one another at Harmony, and he thought about it especially on their first date.

He looked down at her and thought: Beautiful—her hair pulled back in a quickie-ponytail, not quite neat, with some hair still hanging down the nape of her neck. Her lips were slightly parted and her chest rose and fell slowly.

He watched her breath. The breaths were slow and he felt his own slow as his spirit mimicked hers. Reaching up he stroked her cheek with the back of his hand. Her eyes fluttered, and he rested his hand in one place until they were still again. He touched her hair. He thought back to their conversation from the night before.

"How can she not see all this beauty," he thought about this as he looked at her face with closed eyes, high cheek bones, parted perfect lips, her breasts rising and falling, the hips that lead his eyes to thighs that he knew could comfort and envelop, her hands which were strong with neatly trimmed plain nails, and her caramel brown skin. Beautiful. He felt his hand slowly glide over her neck, outline her breasts, follow her stomach, graze her thigh, and rest on her knees. She opened her eyes and his hands moved back quickly to the floor so that their guilt could not be seen. He closed his eyes and pretended to be asleep.

She got up and went into the kitchen. She knew he wasn't sleeping not at first anyways until his breathing slowed and his chest heaved in and out. Eventually he slept. She sat comfortably on the floor next to him and his arms instinctively wrapped around her waist. So, she lay down beside him and soon her eyes too closed and her breath slowed. Yakini opened her eyes just as the teapot started its screech. The night before had been nice. After a couple of glasses of Shiraz, they had talked for hours about what had been bothering her at the club…well some of it. She wasn't quite ready to reveal it all. Maybe in time, but for now the arm slung over her waist was enough comfort. She thought back to last night and how he had fallen asleep midsentence on her chest, the comfort was soothing—no expectations just pure comfort.

The intimacy felt between their words was the closest she had felt to a man in years. She rolled over, felt the warmth flow from his slightly parted lips onto the nape of her neck, and closed her eyes. She slowly rolled to face him and gave him a kiss on the cheek. He stirred some but did not wake. She slowly stood up and made her way into the kitchen.

"I hope he doesn't think I am rude going through his things," she thought as she opened each of the cabinets until she found the coffee in the cupboard and the sugar in the container near the window.

She poured the steaming water from the pot onto the grounds—making the drink extra strong. She was enjoying the aroma that rose into her nose as she waited when she felt arms around her waist and a faint kiss on her neck.

"Good morning to you too."

"I didn't hear you get up this morning smooth operator," he was smiling as he made his smart remark.

A nice way to start the morning, she thought, but instead of letting on that she was being sucked in by his charm, she said, "Your snoring must've been so loud that you couldn't hear me."

"Hard not to snore being so comfortable and all. Those thighs make nice pillow girl."

He smiled; she smirked. They both laughed and sat down for a cup of coffee.

"Sorry I didn't have any molasses in there for you this morning."

She smiled knowing that he remembered her order of coffee with molasses the day they had gone out for brunch.

"So what do you have planned for the day?"

"You," he thought how she might have taken his answer.

"No, I didn't mean it the way that it sounded. I just meant that if you weren't busy or if you didn't have any plans that I could spend the day with you."

"Doing what?"

"Doesn't matter. How about a movie and lunch?"

She smiled at the fact that the plans didn't matter to him. She smiled to know that it wasn't the what but the whom that interested him most.

"Let me get cleaned up and then I'll take you home to do the same."

~~~~~~~~~~~~~~

As she waited, she drifted over to his bookshelves. Her fingers slowly touched each spine enjoying the ridges of some, the smoothness of others, the girth of some, the
~~~~~~~~~~~~~~

length of others. Each book left an impression. And some made her yearn to open them. So, she did. She found one entitled Selected Fragments. It wasn't one of the newer ones, not old and tattered, but it was well worn. Its leather cover, smooth yet firm, had embossed letters on its spine that had called her fingers to open it. She did, flipped through quickly, sampled a few words, nibbled on phrases, and then placed it back quickly without fully ingesting any whole sentences. After scanning a few random chapter titles, she lost interest quickly.

"Ready."

He was dressed comfortably, Sean Jean sweats with all white running sneakers; he looked like no professor she could remember from her college experience. On the ride over, his hand rested on her thigh as Sade crooned from the speakers. The windows were down and the weather was nice, not too hot, and not too cold. At her house, she gave him the remote and pointed out where he could find drinks and glasses.

She went into her closet and found jeans, a camel shade of pumps, and a sheer ivory sweater with a cute off-white camisole to go underneath. She turned on the shower and let the water run until the steam filled the room.

After showering, she lathered on lavender lotion and sprayed on D&G Light Blue. She pulled her hair into a messy semi-ponytail on one side after rubbing some foaming pomade on it to capture some nice ringlets in her virgin hair. She then added dangling copper earrings, bronzer to her t-zone, copper lipstick, and applied navy liner and mascara quickly.

He sat on the couch with a glass of merlot and a book of her poetry.

"Ready," she announced. "Want to check the show times?"

"Nah, we can wing it."

The movie didn't start for forty-five minutes which was too long to sit in the dark but not enough time to grab lunch.

The arcade was open so they decided on a game of pool. That night Yakini thought about the day and the night that had led up to this "date." She hadn't even thought that she would see him at the club, but she was glad he had. Not only because she left before drinking herself into a stupor, but mainly because she had had a chance to spend time with him. The time they had spent together before tonight seemed insignificant now.

Although at the time, his presence had made her a bit giddy, giving her that feeling of being a little motion sick, but not the horrible seasick feeling, no the times before had given her that whirling feeling felt after a good roller coaster ride. She wanted another trip and every meeting they had spent together had given her that same feeling of butterflies. The late-night conversations made her feel like a giggling high school girl with her head under the covers hoping he couldn't see the big smile she had on her face each night they spoke over the phone. No last night had been different. He made her feel special and protected and secure.

It was lying that night on the couch with little room to move with his hand firmly wrapped around her waist that Yakini decided that he was the man for her. No, she didn't fall in love like the young naïve girls claim to do. She had done that so many times before. This time, this time she decided, and her decision felt good.

She had turned to face him and felt the warmth of his lips when she pressed hers to his. She had felt him slowly wake as if a natural occurrence and he simply kissed her wrapped his arms tighter as she positioned her leg over his attempting to find a place closer to him than their skin would allow. She pushed, he pulled, they moved, and balanced on stars that night.

Writing in her journal after the date, she thought of him:

Simple moments with you are made to feel surreal
Your beauty pours out of your laugh and shines from your eyes
Feel completed and contented and secure when I'm in

your arms
Your words are mesmerizing, your thoughts they warm my soul

With you I feel more like me that I've ever known
Parts of myself that had gone untouched for an eternity
You awaken in me when I simply hear your voice in my ear
Your spirit is as near to me as your name on my lips
And mmmmm when I feel your hands on my hips
I am sent to new realms of ecstasy as you pour yourself into me

I feel so connected
Seems as if you were created solely for me
Your body the perfect fit to my own
My mind is blown with thoughts of you as the one meant for me
My sun sent to shine beauty into my dark days
As your rays of light shine a path for my heart
to find love so true
Untainted and pure and real

Wounds from my past your love was sent to heal
And nurture all that is within my soul
Your love sent to tell secrets to my own
Things untold to all others
Your presence makes me feel truly beautiful and desired

Our aims higher than pelvic connections
Your love giving my spirit a resurrection in hope
A new chance at faith in man cause you're the one sent for me on angel's wings
Making me think of future things
    Marriage and family beyond simplistic dating stories
    Thinking on the line of eternity

Of my soul growing old, all in your presence
Of our two spirits merging into one essence
I've decided to love you

11 FAMILY SECRETS

Family Secrets

Not in our families is the story so often told
So innocent little girls turn to women with naughty secrets
We say no one covers our little girls in shame
While touching those parts mama gives funny names
No one touches buds not quite turned to breast
No one is there in the dark caressing the small delicate areas
Little girls don't tell 'cause black folk don't do that mess
Is what I hear mommy say while watching the news
So I keep my dark little secret and remain so painfully confused
After years of covered pain I wear the badge of being licentious
While the infector of my sense of self goes without charge
Unexplained emotions turn into self-degradation
As I embrace all the foul names
Caused by the older cousin coming over playing silly secret games
Touching pee pee places, the one with the funny names

All the small ones know, they all play the game
Not in our families is the story so often told
So little girls turn to women with naughty secrets
We say no one covers our little girls in shame
While touching those parts mama's gives funny names
Not in our families so one sees the signs
The introverted boys, the girls who often whine
The tears that stream when I'm told to stay with auntie down the block
The house where the silly games are played behind the doors with the funny locks
The one with dark closets and secrets that no one tells
The one with the funny named part that has the funny smell
Not in our families is the story so often told
So little girls turn to women with naughty secrets
We say no one covers our little girls in shame
No one touches the parts mama gives funny names
Not in our families we continue to believe the deceit
Our inability to accept the truth causes little girls' defeat
It wasn't that wrong or it couldn't have been so bad but still I feel the shame on nights when I lie alone
I wonder why I let him do the bad bad thing when I should have known it was wrong
Alone I sit and think of the game and the many ways to play
The family dinners he came over and touched my bottom as the others closed their eyes to pray
Not in our families is the story so often told
So little girls turn to women with naughty secrets
We say no one covers our little girls in shame
While touching those parts mama's gives funny names
I close my eyes and say Amen
Each night I bow my head in prayer and hope I can pray
Hoping no one can see the reflection I live with every day

"Well I could wear my dark washed jeans with a cute top."

"Heels, right?"

"You said there was a dress code, so yes heels."

"Well meet me tonight at my place around eight it's free before ten and we need time for at least two or three drinks."

Naomi hung up the phone and rummaged through her closet for something to wear. The club scene was becoming mundane, but what else was she supposed to do on a Friday night? The fuchsia made her skin look even smoother than normal, the denim skirt was short, but not too short; it made her calves look nice, and the black stilettos completed the look – single and available, but the look was definitely not cheap. Just enough skin. The line to the club was ridiculous tonight, but if there wasn't a line then there weren't any people so she took the positive approach to the line and saw it instead as an indication that there would be a nice crowd.

Standing in line, Naomi saw Kini looking at the other girls and thought about saying something, but what was the point.

"Girl, promise me that you're gonna have fun this time. I hate coming out here and then leaving with you feeling all down. Remember we came to have fun."

"I know. I will, I will. I'm not here to find a man. Things are going good with Kyle, I mean no relationship, no rings, but we're just fine. I am here to dance and have a little fun; that's it."

Inside the club was nice. The layout was spacious enough for the hundreds of people not to seem overwhelming, but intimate enough not to feel like a warehouse either. Naomi ordered the drinks and paid the bartender the $16.00 tab. The air was damp with perspiration and the humidified air, which was caused by the machines hanging from the rafters that puffed out huge clouds of cool mist every ten minutes. The music was loud enough for the bass to be felt as soon as you entered the club and the red and blue lights gave all the faces a fantastic, dreamlike look.

"Girl this place is nice; we'll have to remember this spot for our next Girls' Night Out."

"You know Camille and Dria are not even trying to come out to a club. They would rather hang at the house or go get a couple of drinks and call it a night at eleven."

They both laughed thinking how many of their friends had taken on a sedated matronly role that neither of them was ready to settle into this early in life. Neither of them wanted to think of sitting home on weekends, while single at least, or sitting on a porch together gossiping at dusk. They had covered the end of their teens tighter, waded through their twenties, going from inexperienced girls into established women, but the thought of being middle-aged women just wasn't fathomable although they were nearing the reality of it. But for tonight, they were still in their twenties, maybe the edge of it, but as long as the two remained the first number, they felt undeniably young.

A brown complexioned brother with braids asked Naomi, "Want to dance?"

She had promised Kini that she wouldn't leave her alone tonight, and she had no intentions on letting her girl down.

"No thanks."

Waving their way through the crowd, Naomi and Kini danced their way to the center of the dance floor where they found just enough space for two.

The down south thump of bass filled their heads and their booties too. So they danced and had a good time.

"Girl, go on and have some fun. Just because I'm not out looking for a man doesn't mean you have to stay under me all night."

Naomi made her way over to the guy in the gray slacks with the blue button-down shirt who'd been eyeing her for most of the night and started to dance. Not asking if he wanted to dance, she simply initiated and he followed her hips with his hands. Naomi closed her eyes and took in the smell of his cologne, which was musky, but not too strong. After the dance, he turned to go to the bar.

"You want something to drink? I'll be right back?"

"Tequila Sunrise," she said as she smiled and watched him walk away.

She waited through four songs peering through the crowd in the direction of the bar for the blue shirt that never returned. After waiting for the blue shirt to bring her a drink, she made her own way to the bar and placed a special order instead of her usual order of Tequila Sunrise. She wanted something much stronger — "One Long Island, please."

As she lifted the straw to her lips, she saw the blue shirt at the other end of the bar. He noticed her glance and looked away.

"Hmph." She was used to the men who were interested in whatever was in front of them as long as it remained in front of them and whose attention span was not as long as a gnat, as her grandmother would say. She drank her drink quickly and returned to the floor to dance. Space was limited and

Naomi danced flittingly around the room. Hands grazed hips and thighs as she passed through the room, as Naomi made her way back to the side of the dance floor where she last spotted Yakini. She took with her the two guys she saw on the floor who had gone to GSU with her and Yakini.

"Kini, girl you having fun in here tonight?"

Yakini sat in the chaise with a fresh Tequila Sunrise in her hands. Her eyes had that glazed looked that accompanied several drinks.

She smiled and nodded, "It's packed in here though, and it is hot as hell, but other than that I am cool."

"Good, look you remember Jackson and Raheem, right?"

Kini remembers one only vaguely; she had left GSU the second half of her sophomore year and didn't remember most of the people that Naomi pointed out when they went out clubbing who were all alumni. Raheem was another story.

"Yeah I think I remember Raheem. You lived in Stratford right? Yeah, I think I remember you from my first year down there."

She feigned a vague remembrance. But in truth, she remembered him distinctly, hard to forget her first. The smell of Crown Royal and the sound of Prince's "Nikki" flowing out of his stereo, as Yakini waited on her girl Cheryl to come back from the walk she had taken with Raheem's roommate, were as distinct to her tonight as that night back on campus.

Raheem, the brother with the sleepy hazel eyes and caramel colored skin, had used his raspy rich baritone voice to persuade her into having a couple of drinks of CR with him on his cramped twin bed as they listened to the music and talked. His face was that of one that made you think of an old uncle, he had sleepy hound dog eyes and a solemn expression.

She remembered how he took her drink from her and kissed her neck slowly with the warmth of his kiss lingering as his hand kneaded her right breast. The tang of CR still on his lips, and stale smell on his breath, met her nose as he kissed her deeply and laid her back on the small bed while fumbling quickly with the button on her tight jeans. She remembered pushing him the entire time and grunting low pleases stop's no's and the sound of zipper hid beneath the sound of Prince's falsetto voice singing some nasty love song, his hands pushed her pants over her hips and quickly did the same with the plain white cotton panties she wore. He was inside her in a matter of seconds and she never heard the sound of plastic tearing.

Never felt his hands leave her hips to adjust the condom that was never used. He went quickly, huffing hoarsely into her neck, he was forceful and careless and abrasive in his entry.

Kini closed her eyes as she stood now in the midst of the club remembering Raheem from that one night they shared. She remembered pushing him and asking him in a low scared voice to please stop that she wasn't like that that she didn't want to that she hadn't done it before please stop don't and the feel of his weight as he huffed hoarsely into her neck and she pushed his shoulders and grabbed at his waist and pushed and when her nails scraped his skin and cut him how he pushed deeper and answered her pleases with one hard sharp swift jab that hurt so deeply and she could smell the staleness of day old CR on his breath and the fresh tang of the drink they shared only minutes before and he pushed and she pushed and he huffed and she squeezed her eyes and said stop and he did finally but he did not move but lay heavily on her stomach and breathed into her neck.

"Yeah, but I don't think we ever met."

"Maybe not." She looked away and walked to get another drink.

Jackson watched Yakini walk away and asked, "What's with your girl?'

"I don't know she acts all funny every time we come out."

Raheem, elbowed his friend and whispered loud enough for Naomi to hear, "Fat girls always act all salty at the club. Mad at their cute friends 'cause they fat."

Naomi walked off without looking back. She was used to hearing the comments made after her friend walked away. It hurt her knowing every time she told Yakini that she was being paranoid about her weight that she was lying to her. When she felt the hands on her waist when she tried to walk away, Naomi turned around ready to pounce, but was greeted by the blue shirt with a fresh drink and a cute ass smile.

"Thought you weren't coming back."

"I'm here, right?"

As she danced, she felt her phone vibrate on her hip and

reached down to see the text— "Gone home with Kyle. Have fun."

She turned to the blue shirt and put her hands around his neck as they danced slowly to the crooning of an old school Luther jam. His voice was nice in her ear as he attempted to sing along. Later the headlights of the black BMW 500 series beamed in her rearview mirror and with each turn, she looked to see if he was still following.

~~~~~~~~~~~~~

Kini would kill me if she knew I was letting him come home with me tonight. But Kini isn't here 'cause she is getting her nasty on with Mr. Niane, and I will not go home alone tonight. He was thoughtful bringing me over a drink and keeping me company all night, and the Beamer is a nice bonus. I need to call Kini and give her his information just in case though. The phone rang four times and went to the voicemail.

"Kini. I met a nice guy. Phillip Hayes from Smyrna and he drives a Black BMW 500 series. I don't know the license plate number, and he is following me so I can't give it to you. Call me tomorrow to make sure he didn't hack me into little ass pieces. And oh yeah, wear a condom cause I know you two are not talking since you can't answer your phone," she chuckled and hung up happy that her girl couldn't get on her case tomorrow without looking completely hypocritical.

Two drinks into the night, Naomi leans over to kiss Phillip and undo the top button of his shirt. Naomi often told Yakini to take initiative—"Girl if you are tired of being alone, hell take some initiative and get what you want." So she took her own advice tonight, as she sat on the tan suede couch she undid a second button and a third, until his bare chest was revealed to her. She stood and walked to the stairs and waited without saying a word until he stood and walked with her up the stairs to the bedroom. His hands were slow
~~~~~~~~~~~~~

and steady. He took his time untying the string that held her halter to her torso, sliding his hands up her thighs, and pulling down the black lace panties she wore.

He did not take off the skirt, nakedness implied intimacy, and this was no intimate moment. He pushed the denim into a small belt of fabric around her waist and laid her back on the bed where he began to explore her thighs. She opened and grabbed his head as his tongue caressed her thighs. As he continued his exploit, she reached her hands back to the drawer on the other side of the bed and grabbed for the small plastic wrapper.

~~~~~~~~~~~~~~

"Kini, did you get my message from the other day?"

"Ugh, girl I'm sorry. I take it you're still in one piece since you called me though."

"Not that you would even know since you haven't called me since you left with 'ya man' from the club."

"Why are you tripping girl? I forgot and I'm sorry. But tell me about this Phillip Hayes."

"Not much to tell. He is a financial advisor, never married, 30 years old, and good in bed."

"NaNa, you didn't."

"What? Did you?"

"That's different."

"Oh it's different, why? Because it's you or because you think 'cause you went out on more than one date that your sleeping with Kyle is somehow different from what happened with Phillip and me. Girl sex is sex. Time, age, and all that other crap people use to put boundaries on the appropriateness or immorality of it are all silly constraints people like you use to make yourselves feel better. Sitting looking down on the poor, poor loose women like me. Well, I don't believe it."

"Here we go with your philosophy of sex as release. Girl you know it means more than that to you. I know how hurt
~~~~~~~~~~~~~~

you were when Fred cheated. You didn't say he was releasing tension you said he cheated. So don't give me that liberated, modern, feminist crap you tell those men you sleep with. You are just scared of getting hurt."

"Thank you Dr. Kini, but anyways, how are things with you and Kyle?"

"Things are good. I think this is the one."

"Girl you just slept with him and now you think you had some sacred moment, huh? That is so Kini. Girl you are so gone on this whole IndiaArie-Ready-For-Love shit, but I guess you wouldn't be Kini if you weren't a romantic. "

"You are such a cynical misanthropist."

"See every time we fuss you gotta go pulling in some big ass words. Keep it simple."

They laughed off the conversation. Their relationship was built on the reality that two people who were so similar in so many ways had so many utterly conflicting views on life, and especially on love and men. But no matter the disparity in their beliefs, the value for their friendship and their shared love kept the two bonded as close as sisters.

"So he's the one?"

"I think so."

"I really am happy for you Kini, just take your time. Like my grandma used to say, 'Don't fall in love too deep girl you just might hurt your self when you land'."

"There you go again. Pessimist."

"Realist."

"Whatever."

12 SEEDS

Birth Right
No mother in your life
She left you in the snow
Birthed you and left you alone and injected
With the drugs she took
No father
Who knows who he may have been
At 3 months a lady took you as her own
Well at least she took you home
Along with a nice monthly foster check
The money helped with her own kids
She put you out at 15
And you walked away
Your daughter was born on the 2nd
You left on the 23rd
Only 21 days,
A mere 504 hours and some minutes
Measure your presence in her life
Your first-born
Your first true blood in this world
You left your first-born
You inherited this inability to nurture
You were bred into instability

Irresponsibility flows in your veins
Along with the drugs your mother
With protruding stomach
Pushed into her arms
Or maybe inhaled into her lungs
She entered this world on the 2nd
You left her world on the 23rd
Just 21 days after her birth
And only 10 after your own birthday passed
You turned 22 and walked away
Leaving your first real family
Your first-born
Your only true blood
Funny to think that in their absence
Your parents taught you something after all
You are gone now
I am left here alone
Here to be 2.
Father/ Mother
Nurturer/Guide
I must sever the cord of your past
Forbid your inability to cope to hinder her
Growth
Disallow your ancestry to determine her
Inheritance
Forbid your inept heirloom to become her
Birthright
Her worth to be tarnished by your weakness
Yes, she was your first-born
She is my child
She was your seed
She is my girl
Your blood
My family
Your genes
My values
Your liability

My blessing

The weeks, then months, passed by quickly. Her writing slowed to a slow drip of sentences here and there, on the novel at least. Her parents had been calling to find out when she would be "settled" enough to bring Nia home. She knew that in all honestly, she could bring her back now and she should. Being a mother had been all Yakini had known since she was nineteen. College wasn't the experience that most of her friends had had.

Her twenties had been full of long hours of work and long hours of study followed by long ours of taking care of a toddler. This time without her daughter had been a guilty satisfaction. She enjoyed the quiet, the freedom, the ability to make a decision on a whim. She had worked for years on her own. Marvin left when the Nia was only three weeks old. He came back and forth for the first year and a half, in and out for a few days here and there. He called and made promises but hadn't fulfilled one of them yet. Each time she had believed him because it didn't' make sense that he didn't want to be with his family.

They had met right after Kini graduated from high school. She had been an honor graduate with several acceptances to colleges in and out of state. She had her future planned out. Only two months before her move in date to the dorm, she had met Marvin, and they had spent every moment together or taking about being together. She remembered meeting him, so handsome.

Pretty boy with a big smile and a joke for every occasion. His sense of humor helped him to win over every friend and even fool the parents, at first. When she left for college, luckily she had a car and a new credit card to fuel her way the four-hour drive to see him. The first year away at school

things remained great between the two naïve lovers. Time passed and during her sophomore year, her visits slowed as her attention began to splinter into several directions on and off campus. But his insistence on making their relationship "work out" never waned. He bought a one-way Greyhound ticket down for a two-week visit that stretched into an entire semester. No job, no school, no car, he stayed on the couch of her new apartment and drove her to class each morning until the girl next door called and asked Yakini to speak to Marvin.

Yakini had skipped class and when she answered the phone, she was shocked to hear the female on the other end ask her "May I speak to Marvin?"

"Excuse me?"

"This is Rachel from next door. Could you tell him he left his blue shirt over here the other night? This is his sister, right?"

His sister. Rachel lived next door. She had watched us walk hand-in-hand, kiss on the balcony. His sister. She knew who I was and enjoyed her moment to push his affair in my face. The phone hit the wall. The tears streamed down, and he was put out to find his way home.

He hadn't been gone a week when Yakini went to the store and bought the box with the smiling white woman on it. The box had the plus and minus instructions that to Yakini seemed backwards. The plus wasn't a positive in her mind but instead a definite subtraction, a deduction of freedom and future opportunities. She picked up the box and took it home.

It sat on her desk for two days before she was bold enough to even open it and read the instructions. Finally, she took it but she knew the answer before she ever looked at the stick. She knew that the big pink plus sign would be there waiting for her eyes, and it was.

She picked up the phone and called him. It was five a.m. He didn't need her to say a word to know why she was calling. Yakini had called him the day she went to buy the test. He had been waiting on her to call him with an answer. They attempted to piece the relationship back together or at least patched a few spots, which worked as well as mending a brick wall with scotch tape.

They planned a happy family although he had no idea of

what a family looked like. All he knew what that he was determined not to be like his mother, his birth mother who had given birth to him in the county jail and given him up before even naming him. Unfortunately, in his veins ran instability and unreliability. He tried initially. He rubbed Yakini's stomach and talked of the family they would create. He went to the hospital for the twenty-five and a half hours of labor. Then reality set in when he didn't sign the birth certificate. Ten years later, he still hadn't signed.

Yakini had worked her way through college and worked hard to raise her daughter to be strong, independent, and happy. But she was drained, and the messages her parents had left on her machine had gone unanswered. Shame welled within her each time she thought of how she enjoyed this time without her daughter. She loved Nia so much, but it was so hard to do alone. She would call later tonight or maybe in the morning.

The ringing phone took Yakini's attention away from the computer screen. She would write later. Looking at the caller ID, she knew it was Kyle.

"Hey."

"What are you doing?"

"Writing and thinking about my daughter."

"She should be back soon, huh?"

"Yeah, the freelance thing is working out. So it's time to get her back home."

"How long has she been with your parents?"

There was a long pause. How long had it been?

"A few months." In actuality it had been five months nearly half a year since her baby left as she attempted to work on getting her finances in order to leave LCN for good. It had been longer than she had realized until she was asked to verbalize the time.

"I know you're missing her. I can't wait to meet her."

"Yeah I miss her." She couldn't explain to him how she felt completely without sounding selfish, so she kept it simple. She heard him say in a breathy whisper, "Wish I could see my daughter?"

"What?"

Yakini remembered distinctly asking Kyle if he had kids and that he had said no. Did he have a daughter since they had been dating or did he lie before? He realized that she'd heard him although he had no intentions on mentioning it. Not now at least. He had thought about how to tell her so many times, but there was not segue way for this conversation.

"Look Kini, I know we talked about marriages and kids before and that I was a bit brief in my answer. I gave the easiest one, but not the most accurate."

She couldn't believe he was trying to find a loophole for his lie. "You and your ex-wife have a child?"

"No."

There was a pause before he started again, "When I moved here, I met someone and we dated for a while. I honestly thought she was going to be the one. But then I thought this with my ex-wife before her too. Anyways, she got pregnant, but she didn't want to deal with having our daughter split between two homes and eventually two-step parents. So, I wasn't allowed to spend time with her after the breakup."

"How old is she, Kyle?"

"Five."

"When did you see her last?"

"She was six months old, and I was moving my things out of the apartment."

"You don't spend time with her?"

Yakini could feel the judgment rising in her voice. How could he not spend time with her? Why were men like this? I thought he was different.

The thoughts were rushing in and out, and it was too much information to take in at once.

"It isn't like that. I can't spend time with her. When I moved, Paulette did too. Now they live in Kansas City, and she has a new man who Khai thinks of as daddy. I send money to a PO address her mom sent me after she was settled, and I send cards and gifts. I don't know if she ever gets the cards. I called once and her mom told me that Khai had a daddy and that I was causing problems already with the unsigned gifts that she had to explain away each Christmas and birthday. I still send them, but the packages all are returned. Funny thing though, not one money order has ever been returned and every one of them gets cashed."

The information was too much. Yakini was tired of hearing the same old "my baby mama won't let me be a daddy so shit I don't' do nothing 'cause she don't want me to see my child" sob storey.

"Look Kyle this is a lot to hear in one day. I think I need some time to think on this. I can't believe you lied to me and months after I asked you a question now you finally decide to tell the truth. You tell me that you have a child that you love so much but can't see and I'm just supposed to believe your side of the story now. I'll. . . 'll call you later."

She hung the phone up. She was mad at him, but she hadn't been honest either. She couldn't tell him that she was secretly enjoying not having her daughter, as he was grieving over not having time with his own. What would he think of her if he really knew that the woman he loved wasn't as maternal as he assumed?

As they ended their call., Yakini felt emptiness. She really missed Nia, but in all actuality, she didn't want to call tonight or tomorrow.

She didn't want to deal with cooking dinner, going to PTO meetings, carpooling for soccer, mingling with Girl Scout Den Mothers, helping read horribly written outdated textbooks, or even the noise of little girls on play dates screeching and squealing throughout the house. She didn't want to call, but she did want to see her daughter—a visit.

If there was a way she could have weekends and summers like most so called "involved fathers" then hell she would be eager to be the involved parent Kyle dreamed to be too. It was the day-to-day-never-ending-stressdriven-I-can't-take-it-anymore-tedium that she was beginning to hate. It was doing a job made for two alone that she was tired of. Not the little face of Nia. She was tired of wiping noses when hers too was stuffy and her head was pounding. She was tired of not being able to say she was tired because that would be TIRED, a bad mother, negligent, uncaring, selfish.

She wanted to be able to say I don't want to cook or clean or hell even get out of bed and get dressed today, but she hadn't been able to do that for ten years until these last few months, and yes, she was enjoying it. She had never been out of the county; hell she hadn't even ventured off the east coast. She hadn't ever taken an actual vacation. She was being self-centered; but why is that such a bad thing? People talk about being self-centered as if it is a horrible thing, but her thoughts at this moment were girl if you don't center yourself then how will you be of any use to anybody else?

That was what had happened. Yakini had given so much that she had never taken time to do anything for herself. She hadn't worked out in God knows-how-long. She hadn't taken time off from work until the moment when she finally quit. Who knows, if she had taken a vacation or two while she worked at LCN then maybe she wouldn't have felt so confined and quit.

The phone was ringing in her ear. It had rung three times and the next ring would prompt the voicemail message. She anticipated the beep so she could leave a quick I-miss-you-soooo-much message. But no, her mother answered instead.

"Hello."

"Hey mama, I am sorry I haven't called you back in a few days."

"Your daughter has been going crazy missing you, girl. All she has talked about is how she can't wait to see you."

"Yeah well it is almost Christmas so I think she needs to come home. Plus if she comes now it will be a better time to get her re-enrolled at her old school after the holidays."

"I'm gonna miss this girl. She is too much like you were at her age, Kini."

"Yeah I know," Yakini could feel the freedom slipping away with each word that she spoke to her mother.

"Nia, girl your mama is on the phone. Come on in here and talk to her like you been trying to do all day."

"Hey Mommy."

"Hey sweetie," the sweet sound of her daughter's voice in her ear caused Yakini more emotions that she expected. She missed her daughter more that she was willing to say, but there was a tinge of something else that forced the tears to stream down her face— sadness. She didn't want to feel this.

She wanted desperately to hear the voice on the other end and feel a desire to again be the "bestest mommy in the world."

But it didn't come.

Her daughter heard the sobs, "I miss you too mommy."

Yakini forced herself to push away the unmaternal thoughts. She loved her daughter.

"When can I come home?"

"Soon baby. I'm gonna to drive down to get you very soon. I might bring a friend with me if you don't mind."

"Miss Naomi is coming?"

"No, a new friend."

There was a pause. "Is it a guy?"

"Yes, will that make you uncomfortable?'

"No, that's fine."

"How is school going?"

"Good, but I have a test tomorrow."

They chatted for a while over the pending test, all the new friends Nia had made at her new school, and the neat trips she had taken with grandma and grandpa during her time there.

"I love you NeNe."

"I love you mommy."

"Put Grandma back on the phone baby."

"Kini baby, how are things. You got it all settled with the writing?"

Yakini knew that there was no explaining to her mom that she was still in transition and that she would do a few freelance works to keep her afloat until her book was finished. So the simplest answer was best, "Yes ma."

"That's good. I heard NeNe say you were bringing a man or something like that. You met somebody? Is it serious?"

Yakini rolled her eyes; she stopped talking dating with her mom after 25 because every date must lead to marriage in her mom's eyes. Her mom had been married since 17 to her first real love. Most of Yakini's aunts had followed that same pattern, so had most of her cousins, and so she was considered an old maid—although she hadn't made 30 yet.

"He's really nice ma but I can't say yet… it's still kind of new."

"Well have you been going to church? I've been praying for you to find your helpmate in life."

"I know ma."

"Pastor Jenkins saw NeNe and said she was just like you. She's been singing in the choir too, like you used to. You didn't tell me this girl could sang so good."

Yakini smiled, she remembered her days at Bethlehem Chapel and her days of singing in the choir, but that was years ago. Church had become a distant memory for Yakini after Marvin's last disappearance. She had prayed so hard, believed so hard, and wanted so badly for him to stay this time. God obviously wasn't hearing her prayers, and so Yakini initially withdrew from the choir, then her weekly visits to church became annual, until she simply didn't go. Her prayers had stopped before her visits and so God now felt like a distant memory that she thought of at times, but most days she simply lived in the moment with little regard to the future or afterlife. Until moments like now with her mother when she was pushed into a corner and made to think on her backsliding ways. Church was supposed to make you feel hope, not helpless, which she had felt when

Marvin left last her and she left the church.

"Look ma, I don't want to get into this today. NeNe and I talk about God, we know what we believe and we are fine."

"Baby, you need to get back in chur…"

"Mom," Yakini only called her mother Mom when she was annoyed.

"Well baby, it was good to hear from you. Me and your daddy will talk to you later. We love you baby."

"Love y'all to mom."

Yakini lay down. She thought of the day's events and tried to decide how she felt about NeNe's homecoming and Kyle's lie. Who was this man that she had invested her time in? She wasn't sure anymore. This revelation of his having a child was too much to take in at once, but it wasn't the child that bothered her. She had to take some time, some distance, and figure out what she wanted to do. It wasn't the fact that he was a father that bothered her; it was more the reality check of the lives they shared outside of one another. The fact of his having a child was simply a flesh and bone reminder that she wasn't the first one he had loved and poured his entire essence into in a fit of passion and hormones and ecstasy and that she would never be the first that he would feel this with. Not anymore than she could offer his the beauty of being her first to o the same. Yes, she might feel this with him some day; she might even allow him to one day plant his seed in her womb where her body would nurture it until they both could, but she would never, could never, be the first because someone else had been given that gift, that privilege, and although she knew that she was being hypocritical, it hurt her to know.

Not that the gift was ever hers to begin with, but the fact that he didn't even have the gift anymore, that gift of being the first that he could share his legacy with, and that the possibility of that gift had been taken from her by some woman made her sad. The fact that she would forever compare herself to this woman, even when she said that she was secure and stable and knew that she was loved and adored by this gorgeous man she would, and it scared her. She would always wonder what if, what if he went back, what if he remembered that moment in time when he gave that other woman his special gift of his first seed; would he ever desire to revisit that original bed of passion? Would he want to go back to a moment where his manhood was no longer tested as it had been with women before and even with women later, even with Yakini, but the instant in which it had been proven and his body had flooded with heat and hers had melted beneath his?

Yakini wasn't sure how she could find a way not to imagine this scene on nights when he was showering her with love, how could she be sure he wasn't reminiscing on the moment when his manhood was brought to fruition with a woman that he had never even mentioned to her. Why hadn't he mentioned her? He told her of his ex-wife, his first girlfriend, even the woman that he dated just before he met Yakini. Yet he had never mentioned Paulette before. He had not only failed to mention that he had produced a life with this woman, but also he had not mentioned the woman who he found reasonable enough to have his child, to bear his seed, to carry his future and name in her womb and that was the bigger part to Yakini. She feared not the child that had been born, but the connection that had been made to cause its conception.

She thought of Marvin, how although she no longer longed for him physically or emotionally, how although she in fact detested his voice and his presence, but instead she thought of the moment which had made such an inerasable mark on her spirit and her memory. She knew that it was not him that she thought of but it was the moment in time when she surrendered all of herself to him and allowed her womb to become the vessel of his future. It was the moment that she remembered. It was her own recollection of vulnerability and the nights that she would wake thinking on this man who had changed her life for an eternity that caused her to believe that deep down Kyle hadn't told her about Paulette because he too had those same remembrances but maybe he hadn't gotten to a place where he could separate the memory from the woman.

"Hello," she had heard the phone ringing but hadn't taken time to look to see who was on the other end.

"Whassup homechick?"

"Nothing girl sitting here watching a little television is all."

"Want to go out tonight?"

She wasn't in the mood for a large crowd, so the club was definitely out of the question. But she thought that going out for a drink or out to eat could be a good thing.

"Sure, what did you have in mind?"

"I was thinking we could try this new spot I found. Harman's Billiards."

"Pool?"

"Well not really, it is more like a nice bar and grill with a live jazz band."

"Ok well I will meet you at your house around eight."

She hung the phone up and thought that it would be nice to be out with something other than Kyle on her mind. Her daughter would be home in a matter of days, and her days of going out at the last minute would be halted, again.

13 REVELATIONS

Who's Protecting Who

Not able to vote or drive
A delinquent to society his label given by the state
Felon. Offender. Criminal.
The same state that gives him title—father
Has rights to my daughter when the state says he is a harm to the
Yet this same state gives him authority over the privacy of my child
Locked him up away from civilization yet ironically
He is given a haven of protection in relation to my innocent one
The law undone in this contradiction
Who's protecting her from his intentions,
Pay support in financial dollars, they stuff
Money in my mouth muffling the hollers, screams of injustice
So, who's protecting us?
Mother and child while the state reduces
Its expenditures through financial payoff—but what about her?

The phone rang two more times before there was an answer.

"Hello," he couldn't believe the voice on the other end.

"Hi, is your mommy home."

"Ummm," he could hear her talking to a woman in the background, "mommy someone wants to know if you are home."

"Girl, give me that phone." The woman giggled. "Yes, this is Paulette."

"Hi, Paulette this is Kyle, please don't hang up."

"How did you get this number?"

"I called a few of our old friends and … someone finally gave it to me."

"Who?" Her voice quivered with agitation.

"I promised not to say."

"What do you want? Didn't we already handle this? Did you tell her who you were?"

He heard her muffled voice sending the little angel on some random errand to her room to pick up crayons.

"Of course I didn't. I was caught off guard when she answered. She sounds so cute. I just want to see her, meet my daughter Paulette."

"Oh so now she's your daughter? Huh, ready to come play house again?"

"Look, I don't want to argue. I just want to spend some time and get to know her. Why are you doing this to her, to me, hell to yourself? I could understand if I was a deadbeat. I send you money every week, more than you told me to send. I try to call you on every holiday and every birthday, but I never have the right number. I even send gifts and cards. What can I do?"

"Nothing. You decided that when you decided that our family didn't have a future. That was what you told me right. We didn't have a future together and that you had moved too fast with me. So I am simply giving you want you wanted—your space, freedom, no attachments. You claim you want to know her, but why would you want a constant reminder of a relationship that went wrong?"

"What the hell are you talking about Paulette? Remember, I never said that I wanted us to breakup I said we were moving too fast and that we needed to slow down. I wanted us to take our time and we were going to get married within two years, but you said it was now or never. And what do you mean a reminder of a relationship that when wrong? Is that how you see our child? Is she in the room with you? I know you didn't say that in front of her."

"No she's in her room. And no, that isn't how I see her. I see a reminder of the man I loved more than life. A little reflection of you, and some days it is hard to look at those eyes and not remember the days you and I spent together."

"Look, I'm not trying to get back with you. I'm sorry if this is awkward, but I just wanted to see if we could talk about my seeing my daughter and possibly setting up some visitation."

"Hell no, I've told you a million times that you are not a part of our lives anymore."

"I'm getting a lawyer if you don't want to let me see her."

"What judge would let a man who hasn't seen his daughter in five years who hasn't paid any child support, get visitation?"

"What do you mean hasn't paid child support? I send you money every week."

"Yeah, but it's to me. No court sees that money."

"You are still the same hateful bit… see you almost pushed me into calling you out of your name," he laughed a sarcastic laugh, "I actually thought that this conversation could go smoothly, but no, you can't handle being a damn adult. You have to make it all or nothing. Either I am with you as a family or I don't exist at all. Well you're not scaring me away this time. I'm getting a lawyer, and hell I might even get full custody of our daughter. Notice I said our. No matter how hard you try to push me out of this, you didn't do it alone. She is just as much my daughter, Paulette."

"What?"

He was actually screaming with the phone held from his ear, "Yeah, I think I might try for full custody and then you will be the one begging for one damn day to see your child. You can see how it feels to have no say over if or when you see your own daughter. You will see how it feels on Christmas to buy little toys and send them away only to have them mailed back with a big ass "Return to Sender" stamped on them."

His hands were shaking as he put the phone back to his ear. She thought about going all out and yelling into the phone that he wasn't worth shit and that he didn't have a chance in hell of getting her daughter and that no judge in his right mind would give a deadbeat like him a chance, but she knew that to yell would be to draw attention to herself and years with Ivan had taught her not to do that. She tried to stay under his radar as often as possible. He was in the back room, and she knew that he would ask who had called. Not to mention she couldn't say Kyle had no chance she knew he did. He had called every day until she changed her number, he had sent dozens of cards, and gifts on every holiday and some just because, and he had sent money orders. She had sent it all back, except the money orders. She had cashed them. She knew Kyle, and she knew deep down that he had kept the receipts for those money orders. The judge would count those as attempts. She knew he had a chance, and it scared the hell out of her.

"Kyle, look I am not trying to hurt you. It isn't about you. It's about her."

She knew she had to end the conversation, but she had to make Kyle calm down so that he didn't keep calling back and have Ivan ask who it was or worse, answer the phone himself.

"Don't give me that same old story. Let's be real it's about you and your not feeling loved and wanted and your wanting to cause me pain in return. The game is over. I wanted to do this nicely 'cause I didn't want her to get hurt in the middle of a dirty custody case, but you made it this way. Remember that I tried to do it my way first. All I wanted was a few days to visit and maybe a few days when she could visit me, but you made it this way."

"What are you going to do?"

Who has a home phone anymore? Ivan. It was his way of monitoring who she talked to and when. This time, she didn't hear the sound of the other phone lift from its cradle. She hadn't even heard him enter the room behind her. The first instance of her being aware of his presence was the feel of her ponytail being twisted and her head yanked back.

He put his lips hard to her ear and spoke through clenched teeth, "Who is that?"

She knew he already knew the answer. She saw the cordless held to his ear and knew that she had to answer quickly.

She put her hand over the receiver and Kyle heard the sound of the pressure and mumbled to himself, "This bitch is tripping again."

The words came out clumsily as she attempted to sound calm in case Kyle could hear, "Umm, it's… it's nobody baby. It's umm just Kyle. Baby he was…was just asking about Khai."

Kyle sucked through his teeth with annoyance, "Look Paulette, my lawyer will call you within the week. I'm done with the games."

The phone clicked loudly in her ear. She wasn't sure how to react. She lay the phone down and looked at Ivan.

"Bitch, what the hell is he doing calling this house? Did you give him the number? You been calling this sorry nigga behind my damn back while I been raising his child? I act like daddy and you go and call him. What . . . you thinking about getting back with that nigga? Asking him what he's gonna do and shit."

As she tried to walk backwards in a shuffling manner, his hand missed her cheek and instead hit her lips. She could feel the skin slip and the taste of blood was in her mouth.

When she tried to tell him that Kyle had gotten the number from someone else, she felt the fist in her side. The floor was hard when her head hit into the bottom stair. She felt him pull her foot as she tried to pull herself up the stairs with her arms.

The little angel baby stood at the top of the stairs with eyes as wide as saucers watching her mother attempting to climb the stairs with her elbows.

"Go back in your room sweetie. Me and daddy are just having a little argument. Close your door," the words choked in her throat as she tried to erase the look of shock from her daughter's face.

"Ivan, please don't… stop… she's watching… don't do it… she's scared."

The small girl ran away from the stairs and Paulette heard the door close upstairs, just before she felt the hard bones folded into a tight ball hit over and over against her chest. The back of a hand hit her cheek. As she huddled in the corner watching the white sneakers smeared with her blood fly toward her, she thought maybe the judge would set her baby free from here.

The thoughts flooded Paulette's mind, *"Maybe the judge could help her get out cause Lord knows I can't."*

She tried once in the middle of the night to get up and leave. She had packed the baby's bag with both their clothes and left it on the couch like it usually sat every day. He heard the door creak when she opened it. She paused for a second and then she heard him coming down the hall. The baby woke up and cried. He knocked the baby out of her hands that night.

Khai hit her head on the edge of the magazine rack and had to get stitches.

He had kicked Paulette over and over.

The doctor at the emergency room asked what happened to the two. Car accident. Hit and run; the other driver didn't stop. His face said he didn't believe her story. DFACS came and asked a million questions. It was so obvious that she was lying. But they didn't care; her lies helped them to look away. Why would they take a baby from a black home with two parents? So they didn't, and she went home.

~~~~~~~~~~~~~~

As she looked in the mirror, the image staring back at her wasn't the woman she ever dreamed of as a little girl. Not the bruised cheek or the slit lip woman, but the woman who was hit and stayed. A woman who cooked and cleaned and was paranoid that her man might find a crumpled paper towel or used glass when he came home. She had become a woman who never smiled at home and always smiled in public for fear that someone would know that something was wrong and because she was scared to death that he might think that she was signaling for help from some stranger. So she went from being the confident sister who flirted with men just to see the look of want on their faces and snubbed sisters to make them feel inferior to a woman who never made direct eye contact and whose chin was never again parallel with the ground let alone bold enough to look skyward. She couldn't stand the look of this woman's face.

The water stung her lips and her cheek burned from within. She opened the door to find Khai under the covers with her flashlight shining brightly. She raised her swollen fingers to turn on the nightlight and then reached her hand under to turn the flashlight off. She hoped that the room would be too dark for Khai to see the jagged line down her upper lip or the reddish purple tint on her cheek.

"Sweetie whatcha doing under here?"

"Nothing."

"Can I sleep in here with you tonight?"

Odd that the mother needed the child as her protector, but she had to admit that after that night at the hospital, Ivan never hit the child purposely or accidentally again, and
~~~~~~~~~~~~~~

this was the first time since that he had hit Paulette in their daughter's presence.

"Yes mommy, you can sleep with me tonight. Won't daddy be mad if you don't stay in the room with him?"

"No baby, daddy had to go back to work tonight."

Actually, he had left to go God knows where. Well Paulette had an idea where. Why wouldn't he let her go if he hated her so much? He didn't keep her for sex; he had left to go see the woman he kept for that. She had known about this woman for a while and was happy on the nights when he didn't come home or when he called home with the tired excuse of sleeping at his boy's house because he had dunk too much or the excuse that he was too tired to drive home after the club. She was happy that she didn't have to listen to him breath and didn't have to feel his hand touch her waist. She was glad not to be afraid to dream and, on these nights, she was thankful to actually feel that light feeling of sleep while he was away.

She thought of calling Kyle. She thought of what he would think of her to know that she not only allowed herself to be treated this way but put his daughter in harm's way by not leaving this maniac. The phone was in her hand. She walked into the bathroom and closed the door. On the third ring, he answered.

~~~~~~~~~~~~~

"Kyle, please don't hang up," she was whispering into the phone. Her voice was raspy from all the screams from earlier. Her throat was on fire as she talked into the receiver.

"Paulette, didn't I say my lawyer would call you?

"Kyle, I need you to come pick up Khai. I have to get her out of this house. He… he hasn't hit her yet, but Kyle I'm scared… I'm scared. She can't keep seeing me like this…" her sobs filled his ears.

"What the hell are you talking about Paulette? Who hasn't hit her yet?
~~~~~~~~~~~~~

Did someone threaten to hit my baby?'

"No, he has never hit her on purpose. It's… it's Ivan. He never hits her, believe me I wouldn't let that happen, but I don't want her to see me like this anymore. The look in her eyes when she sees him hitting me is too much to take. Kyle, I need you to take her, just for a while please 'til I can figure something out. I know I tried to keep her away from you at first, but when I met him he wasn't like this and then all of a sudden, he changed. I'm sorry I was so mean earlier… I just, I just need you to do this… just take her for a while."

"Paulette, why haven't you said something before? I just talked to you earlier and you didn't say a word about this so-called abusive boyfriend?" He knew she could be manipulative but damn this was a stretch.

"What was I suppose to say Kyle? That my boyfriend randomly goes upside my head for reasons as small as lint on the carpet, huh? Was I supposed to say that I had been to the emergency room three times this year with broken bones? Or should I say that my daughter is losing respect for me each day because she knows that I am weak and that I don't even respect myself enough to leave the man who leaves dark swollen bruises on my face? Is that what I should've said? Or should I have said, ok Kyle you're right, you were the best thing that happened to me and I wasn't willing to see it at the time?"

He could tell that the sobs were real, he could her sniffling and her voice trembled uncontrollably.

"Paulette I am coming to get y'all tomorrow. As soon as I can get a flight booked tonight, I'll be on my way. Pack your stuff. I'll be there by morning"

"But Kyle, I can't leave him. He'll find me. I know he'll find me and if he sees me with you, he'll kill the both of us. He will, he will, I know him, and I know that tonight when I said I was on the phone with you the look in his eyes said that he would kill me the next time he so much as thought that I was even thinking about you."

"Don't pack it all just get a small bag. We'll replace your things later. Call me back in the morning, and I'll let you know what time to meet me at the airport."

14 HOMECOMINGS

The moment he saw his daughter he was in love. He could see fragments of himself all over her small face. He wasn't sure what to say to her. She had no idea of who he was to her. In her world, Ivan was her father and had always been. Paulette wore large shades and a huge floppy hat that hid most of her face. The ride on the plane was silent, and when they got back to Georgia, they didn't have any luggage to claim and the walk to the car was long and no words were spoken initially, until Paulette finally broke the silence.

"Kyle, thanks."

"Mommy, where are we going? Why did we get on the airplane? Where is daddy?"

Paulette didn't answer at first. She took off the hat and glasses and looked into the mirror on the passenger side visor. She touched her lip, which she had tried to camouflage with dark brown lipstick.

"Baby, I needed to come out here to see some old friends and family. This is your Uncle Kyle. Remember I used to tell you about Uncle Kyle, and how he's the nicest man that I've ever known. Well this is him, and he wanted us to come and visit for a while."

"Does daddy know where we are mommy?"

"Khai, look you're a big girl right?"

The girl nodded her head in agreement.

"We can't call daddy from here ok. We can't call back to Kansas City at all. I really need you to do what mommy asks for now, and one day we'll sit down and talk about why it has to be this way."

"Khai, you want some ice cream? I know a place that makes the best ice cream in the whole world."

He was watching her in the rearview mirror when his cell rang. The ring tone immediately let him know that Kini was the one calling. He hadn't thought about her and what she would say. They hadn't talked in over a week, and he didn't think to let her know what had transpired between him and Paulette.

"Hello."

"Kyle, I'm sorry I haven't called. It's just that Nia and I have been catching up and spending some quality time together. How've you been?"

"Good. I have some things to tell you about. Can we meet up and talk?"

"I can't right now. I don't really have anyone to watch Nia and since she just got back home I really don't feel right leaving her with a sitter tonight."

"I understand."

"What are you doing now? I thought you might want to catch a movie with us."

"Ummm, I am kind of tied up."

There was a female voice in the background that Yakini heard over the phone.

"Who's that Kyle?"

"Look, we really need to talk about this in person. I have a lot to explain and I can't get into it over the phone now."

She said ok but she wasn't. The phone was silent…he was gone.

"Mommy, mommy, what did he say? Is he gonna go to

the movies with us so I can meet him?"

"Umm no sweetie, he was a little tied up I guess. We can still go though. What do you want to see?"

They decided on the newest preteen flick that was hot off the Disney Channel circuit. The movie was average, the normal modernized romance where girl meets boy and girl likes boy but boy doesn't notice girl until she gets a fab makeover and looks way too old.

"Mommy that was so good. Did you see her clothes? Did you see those jeans she had on at the end? I want some jeans like those, mom; can we go over to the mall?"

Yakini's mind wasn't on the mall or the jeans or the movie she had just watched with her daughter, but she was wondering who the female was behind the voice that caused Kyle to rush off the phone. Maybe she should've called him before, but she had things to think about. It took her the first two days after his disclosure to get to a place where she was able to get out of her own self-pity over the fact that her man had loved another woman and the next two days to get to a place where she stood back and realized that his past had nothing to do with her or their future together. But how could he have moved on so quickly? Maybe he'd had this woman already while dating Yakini. Her thoughts jumped all around as she considered a million different possibilities of who this woman might've been.

"Mommy you passed it. Why can't we go to the mall? You said that I needed some clothes to go back to school with anyways."

Yakini turned the car around at the next gas station and tried to focus on her daughter. The mall was crowded as usual and finding a parking space was unreal. The girls at this mall dress entirely too skimpy was what Kini was thinking when Nia walked out of the dressing room with the tightest jeans and the teeniest shirt Kini had seen on anything other than one of those LOL dolls her daughter played with only a year before.

"Girl what do you have on? You must be playing dress

up in here today?"

"Stch."

"I know you didn't just suck your little teeth at me. Go put your clothes back on we're going home, now."

Yakini strained to keep her voice low. She didn't want to be in this store yelling at this child. They didn't speak in the car, and as soon as Yakini turned off the ignition, Nia was out of the car standing beside the kitchen door with her arms folded waiting for her mother to unlock it for her. Yakini took her time getting out of the car. She put her arm around Nia's small shoulders.

"Baby, I'm sorry if you don't understand why I said no. But you are too young to wear that kind of thing."

"Mommy, everybody wears those clothes. You just want me to be a baby forever. You still make me wear my hair in these silly ponytails, and you won't let me wear lip-gloss or nail polish or anything. Why won't you just let me be a big girl? Grandma took me to get my nails done when I stayed with her, and she let me straighten my hair out too. She didn't treat me like a baby. I wish I lived with her, anyways."

"Go to your room Nia. As for your wanting to go live with your grandma, that is not going to happen little girl. You are my child. I know you don't understand, but I do what I think is best for you and those clothes and makeup are not for a ten-year-old."

She heard the door slam upstairs and thought about yelling for the girl not to slam doors in the house, but she didn't have the energy to do it. Life was definitely back to normal.

~~~~~~~~~~~~~

Sunday morning rolled around and Nia slept late and Yakini had no intentions on waking her today. Sunday was her day to relax with coffee and writing only, Nia knew that today would be no mall visits, no movie trips, nothing but writing and reading and a lot of sleeping. The only noises in
~~~~~~~~~~~~~

the house today were the sound of the coffee pot dripping and the hum of her computer. She listed to her voicemails. The first call was Naomi: *"Hey girl. Wassup? I was just calling to see what you and little NeNe were doing this weekend, but I guess you two are already out buying the city out of Christmas presents. Call me later."* Then mama's voice was talking: *"Hey there, baby. I was just giving you a call to see how my little one was settling back into being at home. I know you don't want me in your business, but I was just wondering if you were going to church today. NeNe really enjoys going—so if you can just do it for the baby. She needs a solid foundation. Your daddy and me tried with you, and I know it must have worked some cause I can see in that lil' angel you are raising. Tell her grandma misses her, and I miss you too baby. I'll talk to you later baby."* Kini rolled her eyes and wished her mom would stop the persistence on this whole church kick. What was church anyways, all Kini could tell it to be was a social club to show off your nice clothes. And God, well He knew where she stood with Him. The next message was in a somewhat hushed voice: *"Kini, hey sweetie. I'm sorry I rushed off the phone before. We really need to find some time to talk. A few things have happened since we talked last. I don't want to get into on your voicemail. Call me."*

She decided to call after she finished her coffee. She dialed his number. On the third ring, a little girl said hi.

"Um may I speak to Kyle?"

"Uncle Kyle, there's a lady on the phone for you."

"Hello."

"I got your message."

"Can we meet tonight to talk?"

"Well I could just come over to your place. . ."

"Let's meet tonight. Spend some time out together, okay?'

"Alright, first let me call Naomi and see if she can sit with NeNe for me."

"Oh, your daughter's home. I can't wait to meet her."

Kini fumed over his unintentional admittance of not having paid much attention when she called the other day,

"I told you that on the phone when I called the other day to invite you to a movie with the two of us."

"Well call Naomi and call me back to let me know when and where you can meet me."

"Why don't I just come over there; I'd really like to come be comfortable instead of dressing up?"

Kyle knew that he had to detract her interest from coming to the house, "Nah, sweetie I really want to spend some time. When was the last time we went out on a date? Let's meet at Harmony." He knew tonight would be difficult.

After dropping off Nia at Naomi's house, Yakini wasn't sure what to expect from Kyle. Maybe he had thought things out and decided that the relationship wouldn't work and wanted neutral territory to handle things on so that none of his things were harmed in the process and he at least this way wouldn't have to deal with the awkwardness of being in her home under those circumstances. Maybe he wasn't as cool with her double standards as he seemed and was ready finally to tell her off. She had thought over the situation, had forgiven his lie, and had come to a place of peace with the baby's mama situation. Thank God she was in Kansas was the thought that helped Yakini to deal with her insecurity. It wasn't as if she'd have to see Kyle with her even if he went to get his daughter. The plane ride distance helped Kini to feel she was safe from her man being tempted to stay with this past temptress. Picking up her cell phone she called him on her way to the club.

"Kyle, look before you say anything I'm sorry about what happened when we last talked. I know I was being so selfish. I was just caught off guard, but I'm ok now. And, I'm here for you while you try to figure out how to get back in touch with your daughter. I promise, I'm going to support you in your search."

"Well that's good. That is why I needed to talk to you. The little girl on the phone earlier, well that was her."

"But she said Uncle Kyle."

"Long story, but there is something else."

He took a long pause. This part wasn't going to go over as smoothly, he was sure, but he also didn't want her to find out any other way than hearing it from him.

"Well, Paulette is here Kini. She called me for help dealing with her boyfriend or husband whatever he is to her now, and I couldn't just sit back and not intervene, right? So Kini, I don't know how you will feel about this, but Paulette and Khai are staying with me for now."

The false sense of security that Kini had built quickly crumbled, and her heart seemed to implode as she heard the words. She had considered every feasible conversation that might have taken place tonight, but this was not one of the possibilities she had come up with. She had never imagined that he would say that the girl had come to stay with him not to mention her mother.

"What? I thought she wouldn't let you see your daughter or was that a lie too Kyle? I thought you said she wouldn't even let you even speak to the child last time we talked. Now she lives with you. When? Did you move her in right after we argued or did you call her when I didn't return you first call or was it the third call that made you think to go back to her?"

Yakini considered turning the car around to go home, but deep down she needed to see him to look him in the eye and find out what was really on his mind.

"Kini it isn't like that. Hold on let me walk outside to talk to you." She heard the door close as he walked under the garage. "She was with a man, but she called me after he beat her up. She didn't even want to come; she just wanted to send Khai.

"So what is she doing there then Kyle?"

"I told her to come too. So blame me. I told her to pack her bag and get on a plane. Hell, I even bought the tickets for them. She doesn't have a mom like you, Kini, who is willing to take her back. She doesn't have any family left, and I couldn't leave her and just take Khai even though I know it would have been easier to explain to you."

"So how long?"

"Not long. I flew up there a couple of days ago and brought them home."

"Home? So she's staying for good. What does this mean Kyle? Home? Are you back with her now?"

"No, but I don't know what it means for us. If you can't understand what I am doing then I understand if you leave. I will understand if you can't deal with the awkwardness of this. I do, but I'm praying that you'll at least hear me out first."

In the car he turned the ignition and backed out thinking of how it would be to see Yakini tonight and wishing he hadn't said anything until he had her in front of her—what if she didn't show.

"But tonight you tell me everything. No more lies, Kyle, and no omissions of truth and no changing the details to keep me feeling okay about things. All of it."

"Ok, no lies."

"Good."

~~~~~~~~~~~~~

That night at Harmony for the first time in a while, she decided to listen to the entire thing before commenting. She wanted it to make sense to her, so she listened as he told his tale.

"I met Paulette my first month in Atlanta, and she took my breath away the first time I saw her. She seemed to embody everything I had wanted from my ex-wife: she was beautiful, an aspiring model, and completely confident and independent unlike my ex-wife, Kellis, who was always worried that I was out cheating. Kellis was fine to clean house, have babies, and simply be Mrs. Kyle Niane. But I didn't want that. I wanted a woman who had goals and aspirations, and when I met Paulette, I thought she was that kind of woman. She misled me into thinking that she had
~~~~~~~~~~~~~

goals of furthering her modeling career."

He looked at Kini's eyes to see if she were listening and then continued, "Within three months, we were living together, and five months later, she was pregnant. She told me that she wanted to have the baby even though when we met she said she didn't want kids that she only wanted to model. She stopped taking the pill without telling me until well until she was pregnant. I honestly believe she thought that if we had a baby then we'd get married."

Yakini took a deep breath and caught herself rolling her eyes.

"Kini, I promise you, I am not the kind of man to walk away from his responsibilities. I tried to make things work, but when I didn't ask her to marry me right away she talked leaving. It was either marriage or nothing. She said I was stringing her along, but I thought the relationship was going at warp speed, and shit, I was feeling motion sick. So when I asked her to slow things down, she told me to leave. I tried co-parenting, but she wasn't having that. Two months later, she met a new man and moved in with him. She moved to Kansas City the next year with the new family that she'd made. She never told Khai. Khai doesn't even know I'm her father. Paulette says that I shouldn't try to tell her now because she is traumatized enough from how they left her 'daddy'."

Yakini took it all in, but all the information whirling in her head was making her a bit motion sick too.

"So how did you get from not speaking to her to having her live with you so quickly?"

"Look I called an old friend who gave me Paulette and Ivan's number so I called to ask her when I could see Khai. I've been trying to find this number for the longest. Anyways, we argued and later that night she called me back. He had hit her when he found out I'd called, and this wasn't the first time. I couldn't just look away and act like I didn't care at all. I know we have been through some craziness in the past, but she is still the mother of my child."

The last words hit her in the chest so hard she couldn't breathe initially. Her fears were becoming more and more of a possibility. He admitted that there was something inside him that still cared for this woman, this woman who was now living in his home. She took a deep breath and considered what to say.

"I understand," she said the words that she really didn't mean and she couldn't believe it herself when she heard them in her own voice.

"Kini, I promise that I never wanted to bring in all this confusion. I only wanted to call and ask to speak to my daughter. I just wanted to hear her voice. But when I found out how much brutality she's seen with Ivan's hitting her mom, I couldn't imagine me sending her back or even me sending Paulette back into that situation. She would hate me if I did that. Maybe not now at five, but at ten or twelve or fifteen when she realized that I was vindictive enough to put her mother back in harm's way just to get her and not care about the pain that it would eventually cause her—then she would hate me or at least resent me."

He paused and waited on her response. Yakini sat silent, and he was uncertain as to how she had taken the news. "Kini, can I ask something? I don't want to get you upset, but…"

"What is it?"

"Does Nia ever see her father or at least talk to him?"

"No, he hasn't been here, not long enough for his presence to be remembered. He was in and out of our lives the first four years, he would come around long enough for us to think he was staying then he would fade away. The calls would go from every day to every other day to once a week until finally he just stopped calling. So on his last attempt, I said no. I didn't want him playing the whole in and out game, so I chose to keep him out."

"You chose. Did she help decide?"

"She was six the last time he tried, and she wasn't old enough to make that kind of choice. So I did. I don't need another person to tell me how she is going to resent me later and that I don't have the right to make that choice. I'm her mom. I am the one who sees the aftereffect when he leaves. I pick up the pieces and try to explain why Daddy isn't here. So yeah. I am the one to decide."

"Are you making that choice because it is hard for her or because it is hard for you?"

"Don't sit here and question me on my situation because you've had your daughter for few days. So now you think you can judge my parenting? Nah, don't try to question my motives. You have no idea what my choice was like."

"You're right, I don't. But I do know what it is like to sit at home and wonder if your daughter looks like you or if she has your laugh. I know how it feels every holiday and birthday when you wish you could call or visit or even watch from some hidden place just to see her smile."

"Kyle I don't need this. I tried. I made the best decision I knew to make. Maybe she will resent me. Maybe she will grow up and blame me for her father's absence. But I can't deal with seeing her grow antisocial and introverted like she did all the other times when he left. I can't deal with hearing her tell stories that her daddy lives in California because she doesn't want to tell the kids who ask her that her daddy just doesn't come to visit. So no, we just don't talk about him at all. He doesn't exist."

"Kini, no matter how hard you close your eyes that doesn't make the light disappear. He's her father even if you can't see it."

"Kyle, I really don't want to deal with this with you—not now. So let's just drop the subject, ok? We haven't had any time together for a while sweetie, and I just want to enjoy being with you. I don't want to fight tonight."

Yakini closed her eyes and listened to the sound of Coltrane flowing through the speakers mounted in the counter behind the bar. She hadn't been to Harmony in so long that she felt like a stranger here until she heard the familiar voice of Solomon on stage. It was nice to be back in a place that seemed to have such a peaceful effect on her spirit. She listened to a few of the poets, many whom were new but thankfully many were old friends that she had not seen since her last journeys to Harmony before she and Kyle began monopolizing one another's time and stopped coming. They sat at the table holding hands in an attempt to let the argument that transpired only minutes before dissolve. Neither of them wanted to fight tonight. Life was complicated enough, dating was a fencing duel.

But tonight the wine was full, the music enchanting, and Kyle was glad they had chosen to meet at Harmony, this was the one place that helped them remember things before the complications of real life, remembering nights of hand holding, whispering into one another's ears, and the feeling of being caught up in the romantic atmosphere.

"I see some old friends in the back over there. Yakini and Kyle, how have you two been? Nights here at Harmony haven't been the same without the voice of the two of you on this stage. I hope at least one of you will come and grace us with something tonight."

Yakini eyed Kyle and took her chance to get the mood of the night beyond children and ex's. She remembered a scribbled piece of paper that she had had for a while. She grabbed her bag and took the yellow piece of slightly crumpled paper out. On stage, she cleared her throat. She had written many pieces in the past that were intimately close to her, but most of those remained in her journal to be published only in her dreams and were never to be performed.

"Peace and blessings room. It has definitely been a long while...too long since I was here last. I honestly didn't know how much I missed this place until I sat back there and felt your spirits flow all around me as each of you read. Man, it has definitely been a while. I haven't been here for a long time and I thought it would seem odd to be back up here on this stage, but it is hard to feel nervous at home. I'm gonna do something I've never done. I have a piece I wrote for the special man in my life. I hope you like it, but more importantly, I hope he does."

~~~~~~~~~~~~~

Absolute Surrender

He looks down at the linen on the table and fiddles with the napkin on his lap.

Secluded within the confines of my mind
The visions of a secret encounter
That transpired between you and I
Which was so inspiring as to force my fingers
To take a mind of their own and Write

She looks so beautiful to him on this stage, and he remembers how they met initially here at this same place but it seemed so long ago now.

Now despite my attempt to create this
Illusion of nonchalance
These pictures streaming through my
Mind seem to produce in me the same
Sensations given in the encounter
So I am here with my fingers paying
Homage to the spiritual journey on
Which I was sent
By you
Where your body's language spoke
Long divine verses of realness to my Own

He is picturing the night they slept on the floor of her living room with the fireplace lit and the flames dancing on the walls as they talked and stroked and caressed.

Compelling you to bow as a Muslim in Prayer to the East
I mouthed sacred words of ecstasy
~~~~~~~~~~~~~

One in a holy trance
It was far beyond mortal romance;
See it was my soul you cleansed

She was beautiful yet shy. With sheets wrapped around her like a mommy in the making, she made sure to wrap it tightly beneath her armpits, she stood to walk to the kitchen. Once she was standing, she took one arm and moved one section behind her until it was close enough to the other arm to be tucked neatly underneath and form a barrier to give her enough security to walk around him. He had wished she would drop it and simply walk regally into the kitchen in her splendor so that he could watch, but he knew from their conversation after the night at the club that she would not, rather could not bring herself to a place that she felt secure enough to do that.

Made me pure and gave me another
Chance to clearly communicate my
Desires Without once using a coherent phrase
It was as if resurrected from death my
Body was raised, rejuvenated

He thought of the night finally that she had allowed him to finally see her entirely. When she did not hide beneath the sheets or grab for his shirt before jumping out of bed. She had simply pulled the linens back and sat up with her feet on the floor, bare, with an iridescent pink polish glistening on perfectly beautiful toes, and walked slowly not hurriedly to the kitchen and made coffee for him, dark and smooth and strong.

So I am now induced to go back into
My mind's eye and revisit our Encounter
Yet more than wanting to simply
Replay a moment in my mind

I am instead inclined to simply end all
Anticipation
And implore yet another episode
To ask you to once more
Surrender inhibitions
To lay down a human sacrifice at
The alter of physical gratification
And bow in humble submission
Humble submission
Praying to my sun
You are my East

Leaving the club in silence, Yakini thought over what to say to Kyle as they walked to the parking garage. No resolution had been made over the relationship since he revealed Paulette's presence in his home. Not wanting to appear the suspicious, jealous girlfriend, Kini thought over how to feel. She didn't want Kyle to take her inability to understand his situation as her not trusting him. She did. Paulette worried her. But more than not wanting to offend Kyle, she also didn't want to be the love-struck, blind woman who allowed her man to make a fool of her for fear of being alone. She reached for his hand carefully, stroking his fingers until he opened his hand to take in hers. They walked in silence to her car, he opened the door, she got in, and they parted without speaking. In the car, Yakini mused on what to say to Kyle, she knew they would eventually have to talk about things.

Kini reflected over her reactions to finding out first about the child then about the new living situation. She hadn't considered Kyle's viewpoint of this situation; one that he had not created but one that had impinged its way into his life. But Yakini, as most people do, wallowed so much in her own feelings that she hadn't thought how confused and strained Kyle must have been to be forced to surrender his male ego, his pride and allow Paulette, the woman who had taken his child away from him and erased his presence from that child's life expunged his existence as a father from her innocent mind, into his home. She had not considered the pain he endured in living with his child knowing that she had no idea that he was her father. She thought about how burdened he must feel and how much he needed her support now. Becoming a new parent is a world changing experience and to think of becoming a "new" parent of a five-year-old overnight and to be so removed as not to be able to express the love you really feel must be a crushing experience.

As she continued to think of the novelty of things for Kyle, she thought that this was not only a difficult new experience for him but also a truly humbling one for Paulette, a woman who had to come back to the man, the one from whom she had chosen to dissociate, pleading a place of refuge. Kini knew from her own experience with Marvin that too often single mothers gain the hardened label of being the mean-baby-mama not to say they wanted this title or even deserved this reputation but many times because their attempts to do the best job that they know how to do was misconstrued as a process of retribution, of malice. She knew that she had been branded with the same title by Marvin and those who only knew his side of things and she also knew she didn't feel her actions had warranted being branded the only title worse than baby-mama. So on her drive, Kini decided to attempt to get to know Paulette and to support Kyle; after all maybe Paulette couldn't be that bad.

Giving up on the relationship they had was not an option. She had silently prayed for this to really be the one. She shook her head thinking on that. She had actually lay in bed one night and prayed for this man to really be the one this time—she needed some sign that God still listened to her, and yet instead she had been stricken with this blow.

She thought to herself to call her mom and tell her this piece of irony, *"Ma, explain this one; I finally prayed again and look where it got me."*

15 BABY MAMA DRAMA

Can't be Your Light

Believing my patience would last to withstand
The time it would take for your flicker of light
To grow into the glow that I needed
Should have taken heed when I first had
Doubts of her honesty
Yet within my nurturing spirit I desired you to grow with me
Distorted my vision to see you in the likeness I wished you to be
Refused to focus my eyes on reality cause
Within me I wanted to see you be the royalty I
Could see you being
Not conceiving that you had no desire to change
I believed our unequal spirits could maintain
Some equilibrium,
Some balance in this relationship I boarded this sinking ship
Thinking my ability to repair your soul could
Hold back the flooding negativity

Hoping my positive rays could drown out your darkness
I embarked upon this mission to be your
Salvation
Hoping that my light would become your temptation
Guiding you from your current situation
Your current status
Believing that if you and I became an 'us' all
Else would dissolve into the past
Thought my vision for your future could be the cast
I could mold you to fit
Saw the possibility of you instead of seeing
You—as you are
Seeing afar to distant days when life is the
Way I want it to be
Seeing you as a reflection of me
Thought that if I could give you what you
Needed supplied your deficiencies that this
Thing could be a reality
Only seeing you as I dreamed you to be a
Potential mate for myself
Pouring my wealth of light on you daily
Depriving me of what I need
But at the time all I could see was possibilities,
Let go of reality
All the while telling myself it was for your benefit
Refusing to see my selfish motives in it
Now I see that I can't simply instill my light
Into your eyes and expect you to view life as I do
Without becoming blind and stumbling with you
Must be realistic in this relationship and see
That giving your credit off my worth is causing
My spirit to go into dept with worries, pain, and strife
I must let go hold on to my light and wait for
Your eyes to focus their own way out of the
Darkness.

The light over the stove was lit when he opened the front

door creating a small patch of illumination on the wall in the living room. It was the only light in the house, and its beam peeped around the corner of the kitchen and landed on the wall leading to the stairs. Flicking the light on to the stairs, Kyle walked stealthily into the kitchen to turn the light above stove off. The stairs were carpeted, but nonetheless he stepped with thoughtfulness, careful not to make a sound and risk waking Paulette and Khai. After getting up the stairs, he quickly went into his room and turned on his light and walked back to the stairs to switch off the light there.

His actions were those of a man of exceptional consideration. He was new to this father thing and wanted to do it all right. He wanted so badly to prove to Paulette that he was worthy of his rightful title. The thought of telling Khai and having her be delighted to know that he was her real daddy, her father, made him smile. He thought of this scene so often as he looked at her playing in the backyard or even when he glanced at her during dinner.

He had imagined it so many times and knew exactly how he would tell her, over her favorite dessert of fudge-drizzled chocolate ice cream after spending an entire day doing all of her favorite things. He would take her out to the park and push her on the swings, he would take her to buy the latest LOL doll, and then go out for a fancy dinner, even Paulette could come, and then he would take Khai's hand and tell her.

"Kyle is that you," Paulette called from behind her door, not worrying to hush her voice.

He knew if he had shouted in a tone as loud as hers, he never would have heard the end of her ranting on about his insensitivity to her sleeping child, but he kept his composure and answered quietly, "Yeah, it's me."

"Late night, I see." Her voice told him that she was agitated although he didn't understand why. She was married to Ivan and even though Kyle didn't consider it a functional or even healthy relationship, it did mean that she was not his woman and had no reason to be upset with his excursions from his house.

"It's only midnight, Paulette." He could feel the irritation rising in his voice. He hadn't had to answer to Paulette in years and Kini had never questioned his outings, which made Paulette's inquiry even more invading.

She was standing at his door now, "Humph, I guess that isn't really late. Shoot, I haven't been out in such a long time though that anything beyond sun down is late to me."

"Well you need to make sure to get out while you're here. Take advantage of your chance to get out a little. There are plenty of places to go in the city and now that you have a built in sitter, you can go and not worry about Khai. You know I don't mind having her here with me."

"I don't want to inconvenience you, Kyle. I mean I know that you are used to living without responsibilities. I mean… not having to pre-plan your entire day and all and I don't want you to have to change your lifestyle for my sake."

"It isn't for you, Paulette. She is my daughter too."

She put her finger over her mouth hushing him into silence.

"Kyle, you and I have talked about your calling her your daughter. What if she hears you? Then what?"

"Then we finally tell her the truth. You said once you were settled that you would tell her. When will that be Paulette? After you have moved out of here? Gone back to Ivan? What?"

"We haven't even been here a week. Give her time."

"I'm going to bed."

He wanted so terribly to slam the door to let Paulette know she had pissed him off. But his daughter was sleeping in the room across the hall.

So he pulled the door gently and lay down.

He picked up the receiver and dialed. She picked up on the first ring, "Hey sweetie. I'm glad you made it home."

"Yeah, just got in a few minutes ago," he thought of telling her about the incident with Paulette then decided not. Getting Yakini to accept his living arrangement was a difficult task and adding the details of Paulette's inflexibility on telling his daughter the truth about him would not help him to convince her of how this situation was beneficial for Khai.

"Look Kyle, I've thought about the situation and I understand. Well, I'm trying to understand. I was thinking about having you for dinner at my house." She waited for his response to her vague invitation. She wasn't certain how he might take her inviting not only him and his daughter, but also Paulette to a dinner.

"Dinner? Are you sure you want me to meet Nia?"

"Of course I do. I have told her so much about you."

He hadn't thought about meeting Nia. When Kini had told him that she was a mother, it was more like another item on her list. The months of dating without seeing her maternal side made it difficult for him now to visualize her as a mom.

"That sounds really nice."

"Well Kyle that isn't all, I want ummm, I thought that it might be a good thought for you to bring Khai… and Paulette might want to come with you."

She made the announcement hurriedly in one breath. She had struggled with the thought of having Paulette in her presence, but she knew that if it had to happen it would definitely be on her terms. The pause was long.

Kyle wasn't sure how to tell Yakini that he hadn't told Paulette about his being involved. He didn't feel it was pertinent for Paulette to know all the particulars of his life, certainly not his romantic life. And to be honest with himself, he knew deep down that he didn't tell her because he knew that she would make things difficult for him if she knew that he had moved on.

"I don't know how that would be Kini. Wouldn't that make you uncomfortable? I mean not Khai, but Paulette's being there."

"I am fine with it if you are."

Kyle detested the way women had of positioning the

guilt of a situation on the shoulders of the man. If he opted not to invite Paulette, he was certain that he would look guilty in the eyes of Kini, but if he did and things went sourly the n he would still have to deal with being the one who made the final decision of allowing Paulette to come and cause drama.

"Kini if you want to invite them, I'm fine with it."

"Good. Well let's plan for tomorrow night. Seven."

"Let me go talk to Paulette."

"Okay sweetie, I'll talk to you later. Love you."

"Love you too. Call you later."

He closed his eyes and smiled on the other end. After all, it had been five years since he and Paulette had separated. He tried to think optimistically on the notion of having all the important women in his life getting along. He hoped that the situation would work out positively. He didn't intend to keep Kini a secret forever. He knew that she was the woman he was wanted to be Mrs. Kyle Niane. He had pictured so many times on how things would be this time, a marriage between two people who were settled and content in their own lives.

~~~~~~~~~~~~~

The smell of coffee permeated the house and lured Kyle down the stairs into the quaint kitchen where Paulette stood scrambling cheese eggs while bacon sizzled in the pan on the blazing blue eye next to it. Khai sat in the living room with the Wiggles singing silly songs in the background.

Paulette stirred the eggs fluently with her arms, her hips followed the motion caused by the circling of her wrist, and they made small round circles mimicking the flow of the spoon.

He watched her as she released the spoon and pushed her hair behind her neck with one hand. It landed in a long silky cascade down her left shoulder. Her head slightly cocked to the right as she blew out slowly as if tired from
~~~~~~~~~~~~~

the slight movements of cooking. The waist of her sweat pants was rolled down low showing her small waist, tight stomach, and the tops of her hips. She wore one of his white tank undershirts that she had knotted in the back and white flip-flops that called attention to her newly painted pink pedicure.

"You want some breakfast?"

"Yeah."

"No class this morning?"

"Not today, my students are working on some collaborative research so I gave them the day to go to the library."

"Cream and two sugars."

"Actually, I like molasses now."

"Interesting choice. Must be a Georgia thing."

"A friend turned me on to it, which reminds me. I was asked to invite you and Khai to dinner tonight."

"With who?"

Kyle looked down and allowed the words to tumble out, "My girlfriend wants me to come over with Khai so that we can meet her daughter, and she thought it would be nice to invite you too."

He sat back and sipped his coffee attempting to read the look on Paulette's face. She turned her back to Kyle and lowered the temperature on the grits that bubbled on the back burner. Her hips moved hastily now, following the quick jabs she made to the pot that she stirred.

"I guess that's all right. You never mentioned a girlfriend, but I guess I never really asked either. I just assumed that you must be single seeing how quickly you moved us in here."

"I guess I never got around to it."

"How does she feel about my staying here? She must be especially supportive," Paulette mumbled finishing her comment whispering, "or just crazy."

Kyle heard the last comment and shrugged it off. He wanted to retort to the comment and inform Paulette that

Kini was more kindhearted and understanding than a woman such as her could understand, but he knew to say that or to say anything that sounded protective of Kini would be to incite an argument. With all the years apart, he still knew how antagonistic she was with other women. Her snide remarks were not the asides of a jealous lover but of a woman who could not stand the presence of other women. He remembered the many instances that he had attempted to introduce Paulette to his boys' girlfriends only to have her make a scene and cause an argument.

"Look Paulette, if you aren't comfortable going; it's fine. I'll just tell her you couldn't make it."

"What do you mean not comfortable. I'm fine. Let the narcissism go brother—I'm not jealous. Your being with someone else does not bother me. Remember, I left you. So don't get all concerned about me becoming disturbed by your new woman. Anyways, you know I am not sending Khai over there without seeing what kind of woman she is."

"What do you mean sending Khai?"

He stared at her back, which was still turned to him. There were instances when he abhorred her presence. It was in those moments when she chose to garb herself in sainthood pretending as if Kyle had chosen not to be in Khai's life, when she aggrandize her being a single mother and willfully forgot the fact that she was a spiteful woman who took his daughter away and substituted his existence with that of a sadistic beast who beat her in the presence of their child that he wished most that she would disappear.

During her self-righteous moments, he wanted to remind her that despite her attempts to disregard the fact that Khai was his daughter that he in fact was her father. He wanted to tell her that unlike her, he wouldn't let anything bad happen. He wanted so badly to say to her that since she wanted to drudge up remembrances, she needed to think about why she was here, living in his home. He wanted to yell, I'm tired of your judging me, thinking you know better for her than I do, you should be the last to judge me. You took her away from here. You took her into all that drama. You.

But instead, he sipped his coffee and said, "Look, be ready tonight at 6:15 ok. I want to get there on time. And if you aren't ready, my daughter and I will go without you."

But at 6:25, Kyle sat on the couch with his head resting in his hands. He knew that any attempt t to leave the house now would inevitably lead to a fight even bigger than the one they had had that morning and to say a word to Paulette about rushing would be to add to her mood for the evening. So he sat with his legs spread, elbows on knees, palms up, with his eyes focused closely at the lines in his hands. His cell phone rang at 6:45; he knew it was Yakini. To her to dawdle was to be disrespectful and showed indifference for the significance of another person's life and time.

To assume that another had moments to spare solely to wait on your convenience was to assume that they therefore had nothing else of importance going on in their lives. He had made the mistake of being late in picking her up for a movie one night without taking the time to call and explain that he was running behind, and had experienced her wrath when he rang the doorbell that night. She had changed back into her chill-at-the-house-sweats and slippers and had no intentions of changing back into her outfit. She told him that he was not invited to join her in her weekly date with Law & Order and that she hoped he enjoyed his own company which he had obliviously thought worthy enough for her to linger upon. She had then told him good night and closed the door. She didn't need to explain the details. There was no yelling or fussing. Her actions had told him all he needed to know about her value on promptness. So as the cell phone continued its chime, he looked at the number and decided it better not to answer than to explain now with Paulette waiting on a reason to badmouth Kini before getting to know her.

At 7:15, Kyle rang the doorbell. He adjusted his shirt as he waited to see Yakini in her sweats and slippers; but instead, he was greeted by a petite version of her with braids pulled into a ponytail. Looking at Nia he could see fragments of Kini in her face, she definitely had her eyes and her smile.

"Hi, come in."

"You must be Nia. You look so much like your mom."

She smiled a shy smile, and looked away quickly, "My mom will be down in a few minutes. Come in and have a seat in the living room."

She lead the two smiling adults and the shy little girl into the living room and offered them the hoer d'oeuvres her mother had prepared over an hour ago while apologizing for their not being warm with a tinge of sarcasm.

Kyle knew by the tone that she was definitely Kini's daughter. Kyle reached for the remote and then remembered that he was a guest tonight. In the presence of Nia, he was not at home like he had become accustomed to feeling over the months in which he and Kini had spent here in this house with so many nights cuddled on this couch, the couch where he now sat on with his ex-girlfriend and their daughter waiting for the woman he had cuddled with and made love to on this very same couch and suddenly he felt like he wanted a new seat.

The couch began to feel unexplainably tight with the three sitting silent. Paulette, who had as usual overdressed in a super tight dress to show that she had retained her model like figure, a full face of makeup with her glamorized lashes, her hair curled to perfection hanging in long waves, and stilettos, sat next to him on the couch and he wished now that he could someone find a way to place the child between them as a buffer to show Kini that there was indeed nothing for her to worry about in his new living situation. Khai sat with her hair pulled into two ponytails of spirals that hung to her shoulders in a denim overall dress with a pretty pink polo shirt and white sneakers and white socks. Her mother had gone to buy the outfit and spent most of the afternoon relaxing her own hair and the small girl's head of virgin hair. Kyle had wanted to tell Paulette that he didn't agree with the relaxer at such a young age but knew that Paulette wouldn't be able to see his view on things.

Paulette had a smile plastered on her face that Kyle knew was a sign of discomfort, it was a technique she had taken from her days of modeling.

She learned to look absolutely picture perfect in moments when her stomach was bubbling with anticipation and her heart racing with fear. He had seen this face on her many times before, even the day in the car when she took off her glasses to expose her bruised eye. She had modeled perfection and applied makeup to hide the marks, but like tonight, he knew that day in the car that what she felt inside was far from perfect.

Yakini walked into the room wearing black slacks with a black fitted low cut blouse and black stilettos. Her makeup was done in neutral tones of bronze with gold highlights on her eyes.

"Sorry I kept you waiting. I usually try to be very prompt, but I guess tonight is just one of those nights. Right, Kyle?"

He felt the sharp comment she had buried beneath her apology, "Yeah I know what you mean. I have been waiting on ladies to get dressed all night."

Paulette rolled her eyes at his comment and the mood for the night was set. The conversation continued in the living room with the two girls staring blankly into the television smiling at various moments in the episode of That Girl LayLay. Neither girl made eye contact with the other or attempted to penetrate the adult conversation unless answering some politely posed question of one of the adults to break their silence. The adults all talked trivially about countless meaningless events and soberly about events of such significance that the dinner conversation felt more like a panel of politicians explaining his or her stance just before a large election.

After dessert Yakini asked Nia to show Khai her room. The ten-year-old gave her mother a look of hesitation as she had started doing since her visit with the grandparents but stood from the table waiting for the smaller girl to rise and follow. The two walked in silence and climbed the stairs leading to the bedrooms.

"So Paulette how do you like Georgia?"

"I guess the same as I did before. Well I guess things are a little different now though," she looked at Kyle as if waiting for him to agree with her, but kept talking when he did not. "I mean last time I was here, I was between jobs looking to settle down from all my traveling, but I left before I ever really found my place in Georgia, so things are still somewhat new to me.

I'm trying to figure out where I fit in here. I can't go back to modeling, I am beyond my prime in that arena girl, and so I guess it's ok. I don't do much for now just trying to reconnect with some old friends and looking for a job. Are you from Atlanta?"

"No, I'm from Georgia not Atlanta though. I wanted to live a bit closer to the city though. This is close enough to for me. I'm not into all the traffic or the high prices of big city life."

"I guess. But after moving back from the mid-west the south isn't that expensive after all."

"I guess. I don't really know. I've lived here all my life."

"One place? I cannot imagine living in one spot that long."

Yakini felt the tinge of criticism in Paulette's answer. She had dealt with women like Paulette at Chic Noire. She had met the best of the divas and knew that most of these self-proclaimed prima donnas were nothing more than insecure and over-indulged brats whose self-worth was buttressed by their ability to criticize and demean those around them. There had been times when women like Paulette made her feel insecure but tonight in the presence of Kyle, she did not.

The evening persisted while the girls played upstairs, and the conversation bantered on about nothing of relevance, nothing was uttered about the awkward situation in which the three were now living. None of the three mentioned that there was tension built around Kyle's living with his ex or dating a new woman with his newly reunited child living under his roof. No one touched the topic of the indignation brewing within Kini or the envy Paulette felt as she watched her once lover touch Kini's arm lightly as they talked. She could not understand how he could have thought to be with someone like this woman after being with her. Seeing him affectionately stroke the fleshy arm as he laughed at some ridiculous comment the woman had made surged in Paulette disgust and resentment. She, herself, was a beautiful woman, she had preserved her youthful attractiveness, and yet her last memories of a man's touch were those of Ivan as he pummeled her torso and the feel of the back of his hand colliding with her pursed lips in a hard strike. Paulette wondered how this woman could have a man like this to stroke her lovingly, to show affection publicly to a woman that most men wouldn't bother to give a second glance, while she was only given only harsh tones and punches and was now awkwardly watching the affection displayed between these two.

He used to touch her in similar ways. She remembered the night they first made love in his small apartment on the floor too engrossed in the moment to walk to the bedroom that was only ten feet away. He was affectionate and gentle, stroking her hair away from her face and kissing her gently on her shoulders. He was always attentive, and as she watched him stroke Yakini's arm, she could not feel the welling in her eyes. She did not notice the feel of tears streaming down her cheek until Kyle asked, '*Are you ok?*' and she quickly said yes and that she was thinking of being back home and that she was just a little homesick. Excusing herself from the table, she went into the bathroom, which was painted a bright yellow, a distressingly cheerful color that did not refresh as it was intended to but instead suffocated her in its happy rays.

Paulette gazed into the mirror to see if she could find the woman she once knew who was confidant and self-assured and was one who never would have envied a corpulent woman who was lucky enough to have found a man willing to love her in spite of her weight. Paulette made herself feel enlivened by reminding herself that she should be happy for the woman who otherwise would be sitting home lonely and eating some calorie-filled ice cream. She thought of this scene and smiled knowing that the woman she visualized could never be her.

"Sorry about that y'all. I guess I got a little homesick sitting here thinking of my friends back home," she lied not wanting anyone to know that she ever coveted such a pathetic woman's happiness.

"I know it has to be hard starting over, but this is a really nice place to live. Has Kyle taken you on a tour of the big city?"

"No."

"Well if you ever want to get out, you know with a woman, to go shopping or whatever just let me know. My friends and I have a few spots we go to get away from here."

"I don't think that would be a good idea," her answer was curt and to the point not wanting to give any impression of amiability.

She saw the look Kyle had directed at her when she answered and smirked at him. She did not intend to pretend that she anticipated being friends with this woman. If Yakini wanted to find security in her relationship with Kyle, then she would need to know that she would not have Paulette's assistance. Paulette knew Yakini was insecure. She had seen it the moment she walked down the stairs and looked at Paulette. It was in her eyes as she gave Paulette the up-down glance, and upon inspection saw that she may have something to worry about after all. Paulette had made sure to look her best coming to the house, uncertain of how beautiful Yakini might be, and she had been disappointed when the chubby woman with the nappy hair appeared at the bottom of the stairs.

The woman did have a nice face with beautiful eyes and killer bone structure, her cheeks were high, and if she were at least 70 or 80 pounds thinner, she could have the face for modeling, her lips were nice too, but beyond the face, Paulette couldn't see what could have drawn Kyle to her. She was statuesque with a large bust and wide hips. Her waist wasn't huge and her legs were shapely—she was curvaceous, but that had never been Kyle's preference. When she met him, he had dated women who were models and actresses and she had never known him to deviate from that style. She remembered finding a photo album of his ex's who were all mixed or light with long curly hair and all were thin. Kellis was the only one that had deviated from that niche; she had a nutmeg complexion and a short Halle Berry style, and was petite yet curvy.

She thought of the fact that the woman he married didn't fit into his fantasy woman image. Maybe the fantasy was just for that, a deviation from reality, and was not for the reality of marriage and commitment, or maybe he had changed, or maybe he had given up and decided that if he had to choose that he would have depth before pretty packaging.

She didn't know and wasn't sure why she cared so much. She hadn't thought of being back with Kyle, well not since the first night that he had picked her up from the airport. She hadn't seen him since their breakup.

When he met them at the airport, she was flooded with so many recollections and emotions that she had mistaken them for affection. His choice to rescue her and put his life on hold to do so caused her to think for a moment that something still loomed below the surface between her and Kyle.

She had confused gratitude for passion, and that night after putting Khai down for the night, she had slipped into her lace boy cut briefs and matching cleavage maximizing bra, glossed her lips and layered her lashes in mascara, slipped on her highest black patent leather stilettos, and walked into his room to recompense his deed. He lay on his bed on his stomach and she straddled his back and began massaging his shoulders. She kissed his back and nibbled the top of his ear until she faintly heard him say some unarticulated sound, 'yakini'. She asked him to repeat himself, and he turned his head slightly to see her face. The look of annoyance on his face told her that he was not thinking of her. She had tried to get him to surrender to her seduction.

But instead, he looked at her with pity and said, "I think you need to get some rest. It's been a long day." He rejected the proposition of her body as reparation for his good deed. He gave her a kiss on the cheek and told her that things would make more sense in the morning. Neither of them talked about the incident the next morning or any day after.

The incoherent words he uttered the night she sat astride his back and kissed his neck now had a tangible association and the utterance's connection and the remembrance that ruminated within her, which made her feel his rejection all over while sitting at this table and seeing these two gaze at one another, now fueled within Paulette a feeling of such degradation that she was determined to prove to herself and to Kyle and inadvertently to Yakini that there was no way that a woman like her could be overlooked for a woman like Yakini. She would get him to see that he still preferred to be with a woman like her to feel his hands around a slender waist and his hand still desired to palm small perky breasts. It was no longer about Kyle's not wanting her instead it was her need to know that she was more appealing than this new style of woman, that she was not simply a woman to be hit and punched, but that she was in fact still beautiful and wanted and sensual.

The night ended finally and Kyle asked Paulette to take Khai to the car. He held the keys to the car out for her, and she took them quickly without looking at his face or the expression of the woman that she knew would be scoffing at her if she did. She put her arm around the shoulders of the small girl, a direction she knew his eyes would be watching, and walked to the car. She turned the ignition and the radio began crooning in her ears. She waited for him to appear from the small door. Two songs had played in their entirety before the door opened and Kyle emerged with a smile on his face.

She closed her eyes as if she had been asleep the whole time and waited to hear the door open.

She kept her eyes closed for the entire ride home. She heard him singing along with Jill of a long walk around the park after dark and knew that he was thinking of promenading with the stately woman with the coarse wiry hair. Since being back in Georgia, Paulette had focused her attention on Kyle and his home. She hadn't met up with many of the friends she left behind when she relocated with Ivan, and Kyle's lifestyle now was all she knew of this new Georgia. In the time she had spent in town, she had spent most of her time either talking with Kyle or with Khai. And she knew that Kyle's adoration for his daughter outweighed his interest in this new woman, and although an unthinkable scheme, she realized her daughter was her one advantage.

~~~~~~~~~~~~~

It was a long Sunday morning; Kyle sat on the couch with his third cup of coffee. Khai sat in the middle of the floor with her crayons sprawled in every direction and her newest piece of artwork well underway.

"Kyle, I was thinking that I could go look for some work this week. I was planning to go tomorrow, but I have to go down to the school to talk with Khai's new teacher, and Tuesday the kids are out on some Teacher's workday or something. Do you think you can watch Khai for me that morning since that's your late morning?"

She remembered the night of the dinner at Yakini's, Kyle had made plans to go to an art exhibit with Kini and Nia. He hadn't had any time to visit with Kini since that night.
~~~~~~~~~~~~~

The past two weeks had been full of commitments to his class, and it seemed that each time he was free that Paulette then had some urgent situation to handle. The first day she had to get Khai registered at her new school but didn't want to take Khai because there was so much paperwork to be filled out, the next time it was to go file the restraining order on Ivan and of course she couldn't take Khai down to the police station and have her listen to the recount of their last day with Ivan, and now she needed him to watch her while she went job hunting. All of her reasons were valid, but canceling on Kini was still difficult. She never protested or tried to ignite an argument, but he could hear the disappointment in her voice when she said she understood.

"I think I am going to take her with Kini, Nia, and me to the museum."

His face had an inquiring look as if he were waiting for permission before actually making the decision to take the girl with him, and the look on her face said that she didn't think it was a good idea.

"Khai sweetie, can you take your pretty picture and finish it on the kitchen table?" She waited for the girl to pick up each of the 24 crayons and place them neatly into her crayon box before answering his question.

"Kyle, it's going to be hard enough to tell Khai the truth as it is; how do you think she is going to react if she has to figure out why you and I live here, but you are always with Yakini and her daughter? She is going to see you playing daddy to another little girl and it is going to be confusing.

Think about it before you take her with you. I mean I'm not saying you can't… it is up to you really, but I'm trying to think about what is best for Khai."

He hadn't thought about how Khai would react to seeing him with Kini and more importantly his interacting with Nia. In his mind, he only thought that it would better the situation by giving Khai a chance to get to know Kini and Nia, but looking at it from the perspective that Paulette explained it; he could see the possible negative effects it could have on his daughter.

"I never thought about it like that. And, I am not playing daddy to anyone. I'm trying to get to know Nia and that is all for now. And…"

She looked at him with a look of disgust and cut him off, "Getting to know Nia? What about Khai, huh? You should be worried about getting to know her," her voice was whispered, yet forceful at the same time. "Keep your priorities in line Kyle. She should be at the top of your list and everything and everybody else comes after her. That is how a real father thinks."

He called Yakini and explained the conversation he'd had with Paulette.

He could sense the hurt in her voice, but she tried to understand. His dedication to his daughter was becoming one of the facets that most attracted her to Kyle, and she knew that to say anything that even implied his being an ineffective father was to piss him off, so she said she understood. Kyle was the kind of man she wished Marvin could be, willing to sacrifice his own happiness for the well-being of his daughter. She saw his sacrifice as another positive in his character, and it only made her love him more, but having him question his ability to spend time with her also scared the hell out of her. How could a relationship work if they couldn't spend time together—but she knew his retort would be that they could, just not with his daughter for now.

The time Kyle and Yakini spent together became sporadic, scheduled around his classes, off campus lectures, his watching Khai as Paulette worked nights and some weekends, and his revived passion for poetry. He had begun writing again and frequenting spoken word venues mainly on weekdays. Kini often wanted to go with him not only as support but to feed her own poetry bug, but weeknights were for dinner, homework, and preparation for the next day of school with Nia. At times the couple would not see one another for weeks at a time and had been forced to nurture their relationship with inept telephone calls and quick text messages and emails.

After months of phone calls, cancellations, and hurried moments of release, both Kyle and Yakini could sense the collapse of their romance.

The intimacies were becoming quickie sessions in an attempt to alleviate weeks of built up tension and frustration instead of the passionate elongated sessions they had had in the past. And in between the lines of phone conversations was the tension held by Yakini to tell Kyle to stand up to Paulette and tell her that his time was as valuable as hers.

Paulette had gone from asking him to watch Khai while she worked, to telling him she needed a break on her weekends because she had the girl more often than him. She was the one staying up to do homework and to go to PTO and she needed him to watch her on the weekends sometimes so that she could get some time to breath, but he never asked for a break. He felt that to ask for a break was to suggest that he didn't want to spend time with his daughter and the guilt he felt in thinking that he might subconsciously not want his daughter compelled him to break date after date with Yakini.

The nights were becoming long and often Kyle would awaken to thoughts of Yakini's hand on his shoulder and her breath on his neck. He thought of the nights that he had fallen asleep with his head on her thighs and wished that he could revisit those moments again. Paulette watched Kyle's transformation and could see that he was lonely. She saw him retire to bed early most nights, tired from his days of work and tending to his daughter. She had known Kyle for years and in knowing him knew that he was not like some men who required time alone, or the others who required access to sports or cars, Kyle needed attention. He was a needy man when it came to love and affection, and she knew that he had not been to visit with Yakini in a while. She knew because she exhausted most of his leisure time, and so she knew that he needed female contact and was determined to entice him this time unlike her initial attempt that first night in his home.

As he lay on his back with his eyes closed, he felt her weight when she sat on the edge of the bed. He kept his eyes closed; half of him hoping she would leave and go back to her room and the other half anticipating the feel of her lips. She leaned in and kissed him and he did not push her away but opened his lips slowly and felt her head move from side to side. He put his hands around her waist and felt her bare skin on his hands, but his eyes remained closed tight as he wished she were Yakini.

They kissed a long time, and with each passing moment, his guilt grew more intense. There was a sensation to yield to the moment, to allow her to finish her seduction, but he thought of how he would tell Kini, he thought of the patience she had shown waiting for him to settle into his new position; he decided that he didn't want this moment, not with Paulette. He admitted that yes he wanted the feeling, yearned for the feel of lips that longed for his presence, but it wasn't her that he wanted. So, he held the hips between his hands and pressed her away. He never opened his eyes and this time listening, he heard the sound of her heels click on the floor. The door closed a few moments later as if she were standing waiting for him to acknowledge her presence. He didn't. She closed the door. And after that night, neither of them ever mentioned what happened.

16 GIRL TALK

After dropping Nia off at school, Yakini thought of calling Kyle. She looked at her watch, it was nine, and his class didn't start for another hour. She thought of picking up the phone, but considering how close she was to the university she chose instead simply to drive over. She had never dropped in on him at work unannounced and weighed whether or not it might appear to be discourteous. It had been nearly a year, and the formalities of calling ahead were performed now out of habit and not obligation. She decided after musing on the issue while looking for a parking space that she felt comfortable dropping in today.

He wouldn't mind if he wasn't busy; she hoped that he wasn't in a meeting with some befuddled student sitting in his office crying for clarity on some lecture Kyle had given in his African Diaspora Literature course. She remembered the day he had allowed her to sit in the class a few months ago. His intense lecture on Toni Morrison's use of fiction as a way of recreating and narrating African American history with a realistic and personal perspective was insightful. The class had read Beloved in correlation to this lecture. She was taken aback by his brilliance and somewhat intimidated. They had talked extensively on their views on literature and history, but to see him in this light gave her a new appreciation for his intellect.

The door was slightly ajar, which she mistook as a sign for admittance and walked in without knocking. His was back to the doorway when she heard him clear his throat and say in an agitated tone, 'Did you read the sign on the door? Please exit and come back after the lecture today' in which case she did recoil unsure if she wanted to raise her hand to knock on the door or simply return to her car and leave without ever letting him know that she had stopped in to see him.

She raised her hand to knock, but chose to simply walk back in and close the door behind her. He heard the click of heels and anticipated the sound of Paulette's voice and was shocked instead to hear Yakini whisper softly into his ear, purring, 'Professor Niane, I apologize for my impertinence, but I really wanted to see you.' And he smiled at her use such formality and turned to give her a hug. He had missed her so much in these last weeks.

Between the course work, writing, lectures, and the many days and nights minding Khai, he hadn't had the time he needed to sufficiently cultivate their union. And he yearned for the serene moments they shared months before. He missed the day of their self-indulgent stages when lust was being mistaken for love and fleshly feelings fed dreams of what ifs.

He missed the time when they both suffered from separation anxiety if a returned call didn't come at the expected time unlike now when a missed day of calls went unnoticed. He missed the days when a missed lunch call or a missed goodnight call sent questions of doubt swirling. He missed that uncertainty because it fed the need to be in one another's presence incessantly. He missed the nights she had fallen asleep head on lap as he stroked her hair, missed sitting between her thick thighs as she spread his locs and oiled his scalp, missed silent moments over dinner when they only sat holding whichever hand not grasping a utensil.

He had missed her so much.

And her presence in his small office sent thoughts of canceling class through his mind, but he had responsibilities. After all he was a reputable professor, who did not simply shirk his responsibilities to have leisure days at the golf course as many of his colleagues so often did in the warm spring months and the early summer. But as he embraced her, he whispered quickly into her hair that he only needed a moment to walk down to the lecture hall to post a cancelled sign.

Neither of them told any others that they were available. He knew that if Paulette knew of a moment that he had free to himself that she would find some errand that she needed him to do, some teacher conference that she could not make, some school project that needed his creative eye, some store to which she needed a ride. She would need Kyle's attention. Or she would need to work overtime and need him to pick up Khai or fix Khai dinner, so he did not tell her that he could not be reached at his office or that he was taking a personal day.

Yakini rolled over got up to make a quick pot of coffee. He stood and followed her stopping in the living room and sank into the plush cushions of the sofa with remote in hand. When his cell phone rang as Yakini was in the kitchen, she heard him quickly turned it off. Opting to let the voicemail handle his stress, he simply pressed the power button. But she had heard the tune. She had heard the playing of his ring tone and expected to hear him say hello or to mention to her that it was so-and-so calling as was his typical reaction, but instead she heard the ringing quickly cease mid-ring. And when she came back into the room, she saw that he had turned it off, which was unusual. He had never turned off his cell phone in her presence, he had turned the volume down or even turned it to silent, but he had never turned it off.

To turn it off, Yakini thought was to say that he knew that the ringing would continue and that he therefore knew who this caller was and could not talk to this person in her presence.

"Who was that?"

"Oh, I don't know. I didn't look at it."

She didn't believe his answer, albeit honest. But Yakini did not think that he would have simply ignored the ringing. Since his new role as father figure to his uninformed child, he had never made himself wholly unattainable in case of an emergency. She looked at the phone on the table as if an enigma which held some secret about this man. Since Paulette's arrival, things had been strenuous in the relationship, but until this moment, Kini had never thought of his being unfaithful to her. His arm on her shoulder felt invasive, and she squirmed moving her bottom over so that his armpit was no longer on her shoulder, it felt sullied by some unknown secret. The nights that she had wondered if he were really with Khai resurfaced as she sat now staring at the black-faced phone on the table.

She remembered the first Thursday night he was to come over that he cancelled. Although an odd night for dates, Thursdays had become their special day with Thursday being the one day that Paulette had off to spend with her daughter. Yakini had made her usual preparations for the night, cooking dinner, cleaning the house, and shaving any stray underarm, leg, or bikini area hairs that had emerged since her last trim. Moreover, she had taken Nia to Naomi's for a midweek girls' night, where they would do facials and hair until bedtime. She lit the candles around the bath tub and at the table at 6:00 and poured the wine, by 9:00 the dinner was cold, and the wine bottle drained. She thought to call the house, but knowing that Khai was put to bed at 9:00 she chose to call his cell phone… 'You have reached the voicemail of Kyle Niane; unfortunately, I cannot get to my phone, but. . .' She had called three more times thinking that he could not get to the phone or was in a bad service area. She had stretched out on the bed dressed, still in her cute brown dress she had bought for the night, and had fallen asleep. She woke up that night at 2:00 a.m. and undressed for bed.

The phone call she expected never came, no accidents were shown on the six-a.m. news, and no house fires reported. He called later that morning as if nothing had occurred, 'Good morning sweetie,' he had said. She asked what had happened, and he gave the solid excuse that Paulette had changed her work schedule to get more hours. She needed the money to move and the more she worked the sooner she was out of his house. So Kini took the answer although in the back of her mind she wondered.

He had cancelled three more times with the same excuse, and sitting on the sofa with his arm slung over her shoulder, glaring at the disabled phone, she wondered what was true.

~~~~~~~~~~~~~~

"What do you mean, you think he is cheating?" Naomi looked at her girl who sat on the floor with her legs crossed, childlike. "Girl when women say they think their man is cheating, it usually means, I know he is cheating, but I want to think he isn't."

"I knew I shouldn't have tried to talk to you, cynic," Yakini rolled her face up like a cabbage with annoyance. "I don't know why, why I keep turning to you about men, your advice is always the same, leave his sorry butt, dump him, forget him. It isn't always that easy, girl. Sometimes it hurts too bad to let go. Because believe it or not the notion of leaving to be all alone feels worse than staying in a little hurt with someone else."

Naomi sat looking at her girl and couldn't believe that she was allowing herself to be belittled and neglected by a man who was obviously too blind to see a good woman standing right in front of his eyes. Kini had been her homechick since they met in college and had never been one to let a man walk over her, well besides Marvin and Paul and oh yeah Trey, but those were when she was younger and
~~~~~~~~~~~~~~

since then she had never really let anyone misuse her. Naomi had known women like Kini when she growing up. Like Mrs. Benson who was an accountant and was the church bookkeeper, she would come to church every Sunday in a wide brim hat that matched whatever color suit she had on that day, Naomi's favorite was the butterscotch one with the three gold buttons that went down the front. Every Sunday Mrs. Benson would sit next to Naomi's mom and her flowery perfume would waft over and meet with Naomi's nose until the service ended.

Whenever the little girl talked too much or wiggled because of the itchy crinoline slip her mother made her wear to make the dresses stand out like teepees, her mom would force her head onto her lap and bounce her feet on her tipsy toes. The little girl's head would be vibrating on the big meaty knees while she looked sideways at Mrs. Benson who would smile and offer her a piece of peppermint candy to suck as her mother hastily waved the cardboard church fan in her face.

Yakini was similar to Mrs. Benson's peaceful presence, when Naomi's days were chaotic and she was at her wits end, Kini would know the right thing to say or would have a perfect smile to give. She dressed the part of the primly dressed diva with the zest that Mrs. Benson possessed. Over the years, Kini had become more like Naomi's mother after her own mother had given in to the cancer that had grown in her cervix. She had watched her mother grow small and pale, a harsh difference the robust pecan brown woman she had been bouncing Naomi's head upon knee on those long Sundays when Pastor Mitchell bellowed fiery sermons of hell and damnation, purgatory and punishment, naughty women and loose girls, and there in the little sun-soaked church with sluggish ceiling fans was no room for repentance or compassion or clemency or even renewal. In that little church where her cousin, who had touched her bottom during Sunday dinner prayers, now reigned as assistant pastor, Naomi lost her connection to a God that she had always yearned to hear from when she whispered to Him after lingering menacing dreams in scary nights. But she stopped reaching out her delicate faithful hand in His direction when she learned that her cousin had been called into the ministry, as her mother had said.

Why would You call him she had asked once, but He didn't answer. Kini had held Naomi's hand as Naomi held her mother's in the hospital for the three long months she lay there looking emaciated and a pasty brown complexion. Naomi lay for days in Yakini's bed unable to sleep or eat with her head laid on her friend's spacious breast. Kini had been a mother in that way nurturing her back to health and mental stability.

Unlike her real mother, Kini had listened to her in the middle of the night as she cried and sobbed. On a night when Naomi's father was away, she had laid in the bed with her mother. She dreamed a vile dream of hands that reached deep within her small thighs. She felt the lips that probed her mouth as she tried to push it away with her tongue, she told her mother of the dream and the dreams source standing in the pulpit rendering the altar call, but her mother called her a nasty girl. Her mother had told her that she was a bad girl who thought nasty things. She never again slept in her mother's bed but fought her own bad dreams until she slept with her friend and cried a whole night with no one telling her to stop the sobbing or to suck it up, and so Kini was her mother in that way.

"See I don't understand women like you. You seem all strong willed and intense when you're out there telling the world how to fix its problems, a virtual poetic prophet, but let your man be the one in need of being fixed and you can't think, you can't breathe, you can't exist without his ass. All your spiritual motivational philosophy is misplaced. I can't believe you feel like you aren't worthy of being treated well. Leave him. Kini you were fine before you met him."

"But what if he isn't cheating? Huh, my insecurities are my issues not his. And I can't transfer my own doubts onto him and make them his fault. I know that I am insecure about me. And when I saw Paulette, girl I have got to be real with you, she is gorgeous and not to mention a skinny heifer."

"So what, she's skinny, she also left him and won't even tell his daughter he's her father. She doesn't have a pot to piss in and is living off of a man that she talked down to so much that she can't even try to apologize. You have nothing to be insecure about with that girl. But as far as his being with her all the time, that is his choice, he can say no to her whenever he wants to. Don't let him use that daddy crap to cover up that he wants to feel like one big happy ass family. Be real Kini, he cancelled on you four times with no advance notice. He didn't even bother to call until the next day. The translation of that is I'm knockin' the back outta my ex and can't get to my phone and will continue to do it until I know that you won't put up with it."

Naomi looked at Yakini's expression and witnessed something she had never seen in her eyes before, not even in all the times Yakini had trusted the deceits of her unfaithful college lovers, this feature had never been present. Looking at her sitting with legs crossed and reddened eyes, Naomi recognized a look of powerlessness and fragility. It was one Naomi herself had worn in the dark many nights after allowing herself to present her temple as a as form of leisure, a pastime, for some recent connection. And on these nights after having convinced herself as she lay down her soul onto a bed of deceit that she was an adult making a mutual decision to engage in an intimate act, she was left alone. Left alone to come to terms with the fact that it was not an equal trade, but his conquest.

Her friend, who Naomi had always seen as illustrious, inspiring, and proud, now sat with her large legs crossed uncomfortably awkward on the floor. With dejection, she spoke of this man as if he were some divinity. Of all the people Naomi had known, Yakini was the one that she knew would never lose confidence in her worth. Although she was unsure of the physical packaging at times, which was another story altogether that Naomi could not understand. But, Kini's view of her worth as a person, her intellect, her abilities, she never questioned. With Kyle however, it was not that she worried of his straying eye or was preoccupied with her weight or was even worried about his views on her weight. No, for Naomi, it wasn't her girl's unhealthy obsession with her abs or thighs this time, but what bothered Naomi was that Kyle was making her girl doubt her worth.

For the first time, Kini felt as if she asked too much by asking to be treated with consideration and respect. To be called instead of stood up. To have him make time for her in his busy schedule. She was questioning her worth, and Naomi was shocked. Who was he to make her question herself? Naomi could clearly see what Kini was not ready to consider that Kyle was a coward who instead of being grateful for the grace extended to him by this understanding woman, he took it for granted.

Yakini looked down at the carpet and thought of the millions of times she had talked to Triesha about Quincy. She had talked until she was tired of her own droning voice begging that girl to look in the mirror and find some self-respect. She sat offering her wisdom to Triesha's youthful innocence to leave Quincy to find a man who valued her and her time. And now, here she was a grown ass woman sitting crisscrossed on the floor telling her girl how her man isn't ignoring her he is just busy, really really busy.

~~~~~~~~~~~~~

She looked at the black face of the phone and glanced at his face. He glimpsed her look up and misread it as a look of adoration and smiled; she didn't.
~~~~~~~~~~~~~

17 VALIDITY

The nights that Kyle didn't call or come by became more frequent and the length of time between the visits more spread out. Yakini wrote; it became her method of diversion from the intense loneliness she felt knowing that he was nurturing someone other than herself. She felt guilty knowing that she envied a child. She wished for the attention, the time, and the absolute adoration he poured on the child, and she felt ashamed, shame was the feeling that resonated within her. Her neediness created within her embarrassment because she recognized that it was right and it was beautiful that he loved his daughter so much.

She cringed thinking that her own insecurities caused her to want him to restrain his feeling of enchantment that came with new fatherhood just so that she could feel significant. So, she used her words as a buffer to her feelings. She wrote. She spent time with Nia, she took up meditation. But mainly she wrote. After getting Nia sent off to bed, checking homework, and cleaning dinner dishes, she sat down, opened the file suitably named novel file, and wrote.

As the words filled the screen and quickly became pages, she was astonished at how much she had accomplished during those nights. Not that she didn't miss Kyle, but it was good to see her goal becoming a reality. His absence came with her own growth. Writing entire chapters in one sitting, she would sit and write until she had drained her mind, or her body was simply too exhausted to stay up any longer.

After waking in the mornings and driving Nia to school, she would sit again with coffee in hand and type more words. Many she kept and many she erased, some she changed, but they all rushed out. Her novel was near completion far before her projected date. She was sure her agent, whom Yakini had not called in months, had given up on the novel, again. Jamison had observed this cycle many times; Yakini had called on numerous occasions to tell her that she was picking it up again. So often had this happened that Jamison had stopped seeking out possible publishing companies. She waited instead for the call that another postponement was needed or that a new direction had been taken and more time therefore was needed, but the call of completion, that was a new part to this process. Jamison was really a good agent. She had tried to be optimistic the first three years of waiting for Yakini to finish the book after all Yakini had produced a multitude of articles and essays that all moved quickly. With the novel this time, Jamison again tried to be the cheerleader the first few months. She kept reminding Yakini of how grand it would be to finally finish something that was totally her own creation, to feel ownership of her creativity again, but finally she tired of the calls, and the notes, and eventually even the emails.

"Well, Yakini I didn't know that you were working on it again. I mean you called of course and said you were, but you know how that usually goes. It's great that you finished it. I have to honest with you , your project hasn't been on the top of my list of priorities. The authors that have been producing actual work, for those I have publishing houses lined up to talk, but as for your novel, hell I don't even know what this one is about. I mean not to sound skeptical, but I know that you aren't with La Chic Noire. I have to let you know up front that I can't just push a piece of rubbish that you finished in a hurry just to get you paid. My name has credibility, and I want to keep it that way."

"Jamison, not to sound smug, but I have a name too. I am known for quality work, and like you, I want to keep it that way. And by the way, I left La Chic Noire remember. As for money, I am not pressed for finances. But back to what the book, it's, let's say, fictionalized autobiographical exposé. Mainly I dish on why I left the magazine, what the concept of it was and the commercialized idiocy into which it has transformed due to greed and power."

"Send a copy; I'll get to it next week."

"It should be there before then, I already put it in the mail."

18 SISTER LOVE

Progress

Movement in this thing called life
In and out they go
Passing through or sitting for a chat
But never simply staying
Never permanent
Never immobile
In this life thing
There is movement
Quick or slow
Invisible to the naked eye
Slight shifts
Strong enough to quake the earth
Drastic tumbles
Movements
Move
Going, walking, running, rolling
Singing, talking, crying, wailing
Action, passion
Feeling, emotion
In this life thing
All things move

In the movement of life
Cycles and revolution
Angles and curves
Curves
Bodies in motion
Lives in action
Stagnancy not permissible
Accumulation or improvement
Loss or degeneration
Generation after generation
Grandmother to daughter to granddaughter
Movement
Sisters
Move
Action

With the novel finished, the relationship and its direction filled her thoughts. She had considered calling Kyle, but decided against it. Instead she, walked into the bathroom and pulled down the white cotton briefs in hopes of a scarlet smear, but the stark whiteness stared back at her for the twenty-eighth day of its invasion. She had not talked to Kyle in two and a half weeks, making certain to avoid his calls and driving out of the way to ensure not passing him on her way to any destination. Harmony was no longer her haven, but had become instead a place to be dodged. The red absence was a scary thought. She thought back to how she felt when Nia was away, the pure freedom that she had savored so much. She had come to terms with the fact that this might be a part of her life, and the pending sessions of late-night feedings or teething horrors loomed ahead. She had gone to buy a home test three times and walked out each time not wanting to be certain. Certainty had its drawbacks.

He had left dozens of messages, none of which had been returned. The last one seemed final, three days ago. He said he understood that she felt frustrated and unappreciated and that he knew that she needed more than he had to offer right now and that he would not bother her, but he would be open to listen when she was ready to talk. He hung up, with no 'love you sweetie' or 'miss you'.

Naomi had called, but Yakini did not answer. She did not want to deal with the cynical wise cracks on love and men and the 'girl you know he's cheating anyway' comments. She didn't want to be chastised for possibly being pregnant and hearing Naomi talk about how safe sex is the only sex and how she shouldn't have been going unprotected with a man whose faithfulness was uncertain, and what the hell were you thinking girl don't you know there are things out there that a pill won't clear up in a few days.

The ringing phone continued, and Kini did not bother to look to see who was calling. She would listen to the message later. She dialed her voicemail and listened: "Yakini I finished the manuscript the other day, and I have to say I am impressed. I have been shopping you around to a few publishing houses, and well call me and we will have to talk about when to go look over some offers I received on your project. Congratulations girl, I honestly have to tell you that I had almost lost hope in this book. But call me soon, real soon."

Yakini listened to it three times before returning Jamison's call. Since leaving the magazine, she hadn't considered any real course to take with her writing, the freelance grind kept her finances flowing, but Kini never considered it her ultimate ambition. The novel was always a distant dream, but she had never actually pictured this moment and living it now seemed so surreal. Her novel was going to be published, which didn't mean automatic success, but it did mean something, didn't it? Yakini thought about the meaning of it, which until listening to this message had played out in her imagination a million different ways. She had pictured a myriad of possibilities ranging from instantaneous commercial success to academic approval but no pecuniary rewards, to supermarket checkout reading displays between tabloids and lotto numbers, and on to the chance of her efforts turning out to be one or two dusty copies hanging stagnantly in some obscure bookstore. She had dreamed it, but never considered the reality of it.

"Jamison Hartley, please."

The monotonous melody of hold music, which was a compilation of eighties soft rock and R&B, played for several minutes before anyone answered. Jamison shared her various ideas on how she wanted the project promoted. She said it was all about the marketing from this point on. They would meet over dinner the following night to discuss the details. The lecturing tour was the thing that worried Yakini the most. Although she had fantasized of traveling from city to city years ago, the thought of going out unaccompanied with only her belongings and her novel to keep her company frightened her.

Initially she contemplated taking Nia with her, but Jamison recommended that the tour's hectic schedule wouldn't permit adequate time to care for a child. Kini thought of hiring a nanny to go with her on the tour, but again Jamison advised Kini that the company would not spend money that it had not yet made and although Kini had saved for being out of work for an extended amount of time, a full-time nanny had not been budgeted into the picture. Nia would have to go back with her grandparents for a little more time.

Nia didn't dispute the decision; she liked staying with her grandparents where she would be permitted to do many of the things her mother withheld from her young grasp. Her friends at her new school back near her grandparents would be there waiting for her return that she had told them would come soon. She had begged her mother initially to allow her to return to the school to finish out the school year but had been forced to come home. Turning eleven before the new term, she knew that middle school with her grandma would definitely be much better than dealing with her mom's strict rules. She didn't want any more braids and twists ever day, and she definitely had no intentions of rocking that nappy afro or those two puffs her mom thought were so cute. Nia thought about the possibility of living with her grandma. Her grandma told her when she was down there last time that she was going take her to the salon and get her hair straightened out finally. Nia even bet her grandmother would take her to get those jeans that her mom claimed were too tight. Grandma understood that Nia didn't want to look like a tomboy, and she even knew that every girl should have her ears pierced and wear lip-gloss.

"Are you sure you don't mind going back to grandma's for a little while Nia? I don't have to go you know, or I can go later. Just say the word and I'll stay no."

"Mom, you have worked on this thing forever and I don't want to be the reason you don't go platinum or get a Grammy or something."

"Books don't go platinum baby they…"

"Whatever they do, I want yours to do it. So go, plus I can tell the kids that my mom is famous now. A tour, yeah that sounds famous."

"Girl you are a trip, always looking for what you can get outta something."

They smiled and hugged but deep down Yakini felt the same sickening feeling she felt back when she enjoyed her daughter's absence. She questioned her motherly instincts and wondered if Nia sensed her inadequacies. She was growing so fast. Eleven already.

19 REDIRECTION

Black suite, red silk top, ruby red pumps, red clutch, bronze leather jacket, ivory sweater, straight leg jeans, black stiletto boots, chocolate slacks, pink button down, chocolate fedora, caramel sling backs, she packed her bag and looked in the closet for more casual clothing, most of which was too little now. Her closet was filled to the brim with jeans she had worn four years ago with a promise that she would lose weight and get back into them, sweaters that pressed her breast as flat as the best sports bra, and dresses that showed each and every roll she had on her back. Four more outfits and that was it. She could mix it up from there. Anyways they wouldn't fit much longer anyways. She simply buy things on the road. The first month or so she didn't put on any weight, and so far, this month only a couple of pounds, but she knew that was only the start.

The messages from Kyle came infrequently now and with less urgency in his voice. She had thought of calling him to tell all about her book and leaving town but decided that it was best not to call. What would she say when they talked? She couldn't deal with second place and with his current situation she had been settling for third most days and fourth of fifth if his job had any urgent needs. She was tired of crying into her pillow and feeling lonely while in a relationship. If she was going to cry over being lonely, she would be just that…alone. No more involved separately crap.

They lived too close to settle for a long-distance relationship and if he didn't feel their relationship warranted his time, then she didn't feel her time warranted their relationship any longer. She sealed the envelope to his letter.

She explained the book deal, the tour, the pregnancy, and the pending termination. She didn't want his opinion, judgment, or guilt. Her cell phone rang. Naomi. Darn, how could I have forgotten to call my ace?

"Hey homechick."

"So what are we getting into tonight?"

"NaNa, girl I am so sorry. I guess I have been so busy and excited that I forgot to call you. I am leaving town for a little while."

"Leaving? Girl shut up, where the hell are you going? Visiting mom and dad?"

"The book. Look, you know the book, right? Well, I finished it a few weeks ago and sent it off to Jamison. Well girl she got someone to actually publish it. I have to leave to do some promotions. You know Jamison is serious with marketing, so I have to leave right away. I really meant to call."

"When does it come out girl?"

"Not for a few months, but Jamison is sending me on a tour to get my face out and to do some speaking in a few spots so that my name won't be so new when it actually comes out. But I leave tomorrow."

"Tomorrow? You weren't going to call me Kini? You talk all this shit about sharing and being real and then you just plan to leave and not say a word. What is with that?"

Naomi sat on the edge of the bed and listened to her girl. She knew that they hadn't talked as much, but a tour for months and she didn't think to call. I bet she called that negro though, "So what does Kyle think?"

"I don't know. I haven't talked to him."

"So you were just going to leave everybody, huh? Just up and go and not tell anybody? I have read every freakin' version of that book. I listened to you read twenty-two chapters over the phone and you didn't think to call me?"

"NaNa girl you know it isn't like that, right?"

"Look girl, don't sweat it. I hope you have a safe trip alright, but I I have another call coming in. I have to go."

"NaNa."

"I'll talk to you soon."

The phone went silent in Yakini's ear.

20 CATHARSIS

Lying on his back, he counted the marks on the ceiling. The painters had duplicated the swirls repeatedly using identical tools to create hundreds of similar yet distinctive embossment in the plaster. The phone rang in his ear; this was his fifth call today. He strained to remember their last conversation. Maybe it was how he had looked at her when she walked in to the office that gave her the impression that he didn't want her there. No, that didn't make any sense they had spent the entire afternoon together that day. The phone call he made to her the next morning was the usual good-morning-have-a-nice-day-I-miss-you-love-you-talk-to-you-later-call, but then she didn't call. He had really meant to pick up the phone to call her again, but Khai had a fever and the next four days he had stayed home with her—Strep throat and tonsillitis—he had meant to call Yakini and now he thought about how she may have taken his nonchalance.

But in reality, he knew now that he didn't call for the same reason he had stopped calling her in the first months of the relationship, he knew she would call, he expected her to call, and it never crossed his mind that he should need to pick up the phone and call because eventually, she always called, well at least before this time. Months had passed since they had talked; three months and six days, he had called every day initially he had called every morning as he had since the start of things when they would wake each other with raspy morning voices and giggles. Over the past weeks, he had called every night finally dozing off conceding with the fact that she was not calling.

Her voice mail picked up again and he left another rambling message, "Yakini, it's me Kyle. I hope you are ok. I miss you and um I guess I just want to make sure you are ok or alive, but I guess you are because your phone is still on and so you must be at least able to pay the phone bill, so you aren't hurt or sick but anyways when you get this call me or just come by or something. Um bye, I hope I hear from you soon." He hung up the phone and continued counting the plaster vortexes but gave up after realizing he had counted the same row twice at least and, who knows how many times he had recounted actual swirls. So, he closed his eyes and at three he woke up and started the count over.

~~~~~~~~~~~~~

Café Harmony was filled on Wednesday with poets waiting to take the stage, Kyle signed his name and s at smoking a cigar and sipped on a cognac while he waited to hear his name called. He flipped through the pages to find some inspiration before mounting the stage tonight. He had written so much, but not one of these pieces did he plan to share as he had sat up for the past months scrawling them into his journal after his eyes had tired of the plaster bends on the ceiling. As he flipped the pages, hoping to find one he was willing to read, he saw Naomi and hoped to see Kini follow behind, but he didn't.

He had thought to call Naomi to ask about her girl, but to call her girl was to admit one that something had gone wrong and two that he had been played. He would talk to
~~~~~~~~~~~~~

her after he finished the poem. He'd keep it simple, "How's your girl?" He couldn't ask where she was, admitting that she had abandoned the relationship and left him waiting aimlessly. When Solomon called his name, he looked over to Naomi's table again in some hopes that Kini might be there, and to see if Naomi's expression demonstrated some indication of sentiment at the sound of his name. She looked up and smiled at him. He gave a quick nod in her direction and went to the stage.

"Peace and blessings, Harmony. I have been back in here a lot lately reading my older pieces, but I guess I will do this one tonight. I see an old friend out there, Naomi Carter. I hope she'll do me the favor of listening to this piece and passing it on to the ears I hoped could have been here to hear it.

My Journey to Solitude

In the midst of the boom of bass and the pouring out of minds
A conversation was invoked between the flashing lights and smoke
Asked profound questions
Made some spellbinding statements and I
Simply took you in
Took deep breaths of you inhaled your essence
This was the moment that I knew I could lasso comets and hopscotch on
stars
Felt like I could play Double Dutch with rainbows
While angels commanded my moves
Night one, we said our goodbyes with a hope
Sealed that this would be the realest love, lust, or connection
Whatever happened to come of this chance meeting
Calls began and I could feel your spirit in my ear
Each time my name rolled off your tongue

Felt your breath on my cheek when I was alone
And I could close my eyes and feel my hands on your waist
Gave me intoxicating scenes of you and I
Together throughout infinity watching the coming of a new earth
In each conversation, seeds planted into minds that led to
The birth to a constellation of dreams
Where I became your sun attempting to light
Your path and you became my moon and
Began to shine off my smile and I began to smile your smile on my face
But then time passed
Initially you were pleased with our constant conversation
Our sporadic passionate mind altering
Physical visitations
Pleased with being needed although more sexually than spiritually
I thought that physical gratification was synonymous to intimacy
So we lay down on a bed of charm and allowed our spirits to be caressed
You put your energy into pleasing me physically and your femininity
Was unique from all the others from the past
But I know your soul began to feel neglected,
Spirit felt rejected as I only spoke of physical desires
But I know my soul's desire was for our aim to be higher than
Pelvic connections
In yearning for a spiritual rejuvenation you pleaded for time
With time being the equivalent to worth
And I am sorry that I granted you a meager allowance
On which to try to nurture your needs
You desired to be needed mentally

Yearned for emotionally
Cared for in entirety and I can see now
That you only wanted me to come back again
And journey with you as we had the first night
When we met in smoke and lights
You needed true intimacy
You dreamed into the end that I would simply
Decide to come with you make the choice that
All else would be put on hold until I could first
Reunite with you spiritually
Get past our status of sexual complacency and
Get onto fulfilling one another's holistic needs
You needed me to see that if I gave you
Mentalgasms
Where my thoughts probe your ideas
And your dreams screamed my name
That we could get back to emotional
Satisfaction
Where my feeling would hold your desires and
Your desires would caress my tears
And stroke my smile
And your spirit could scream my name
You thought then that things could return to that moment
In time when you and I sat on the edge of the universe
Dangled our feet in the Milky Way
But I chose to simply stay
And continue to
Exploit love
I know you looked back for me to follow you
As you journeyed out of stagnancy
You looked back every few feet as I walked
Past our bed of Falsity where physical sensations
Were made to feel like emotional growth
You looked back to see if I would follow
As you walked past those stars that now seem too
Far away

You said prayers to guide me your way
You used memories of our intimacies to regain
A false sense of reality where our love had
Sustenance that nourished our spirits
You told yourself that it could again be like the first night
But I did not follow your trail of tears but sat
Bu stroked my own bruised ego
As if the fleshly rendezvous were actually comparable
To the Soul fusion we needed
So I sat and stroked my ego watching you go
Not following the path of light that still shone for me
only
I sat and watched your feet beat a path in the earth
Walking in circles at times
I watched you walk the earth lighting signal fires for me
Thinking I was lost and wanting
To make sure to leave a way for me
To find you when it was time
But I wasn't lost physically
I was spellbound with sexuality
And I could not see that it did not equal love
So I sat and stroked my male ego
Played with my masculinity
I believed that to follow you would be
To forsake all that made me strong and manly
All the while, you lit stars and begged mother earth
To send me fireflies to guide me to you
Their lights have extinguished and I only wish
I could go back for you
To regain our balance so that we can scale the stars
together
Sky walk on clouds
So that we can balance on mountaintops
I pray that you will hear these words
And feel their beat
So that you and I can dance one more time
Cheek to cheek and feel the bass boom

And the snare beat
As our feet move to
The tempo of love

~~~~~~~~~~~~~~

Hmph, I have always thought those heartbroken take me back baby please baby baby please poets were weak and also a bit pathetic on stage begging for redemption in the presence of strangers. But I feel redeemed as I walk off stage. Even though she couldn't hear the words, their release into the atmosphere was a necessity.

"Hey girl. Long time, how have you been?"

She is sitting alone at Harmony, which is odd. Naomi wasn't the poetic type; in fact, she wasn't into poetry at all. He remembered a conversation they had had at a dinner party where she explained to Kini that although she supported Kini's we-are-the-world, words-set-you-free-mentality because Kini was her girl that overall she thought this whole poetry club scene was too self-aggrandizing for her.

With the music and the poet on stage, she misunderstood his question and answered, "She's good. Enjoying the tour and all. She is in Cincinnati until Friday morning I think. I can't wait to see her though. I bet she's showing by now, but I am sure you have plenty of pictures." She saw the look of uncertainty on his face and knew immediately that she had revealed something new to him.

"She didn't tell you; did she?"

"What tour? Naomi I haven't talked to Yakini in months. She won't return my calls. I call her at least twice a day, and she hasn't called me back once. I thought things were ok between us, I mean not perfect but damn not leave town and not tell me bad."

"So, you haven't spoken since she left town, so you don't know huh? The book is coming out soon. Her agency sent her out on a lecture circuit to get her name out before the
~~~~~~~~~~~~~~

release date." Naomi was shocked that Kini hadn't said a word about having broken up with Kyle. Every time Naomi had asked how things are, she said that everything was fine.

"I guess maybe I shouldn't be talking to you about all her business and all. I mean, that's my girl. Give her a call; she'll be home in a couple of weeks."

"Hmph," he looked completely dejected, "out of town all this time. I mean the last time we hung out everything was fine. But then all of a sudden she stopped answering her phone and wouldn't return my calls. I thought maybe something was wrong with Nia or she had to go home to check on family issues."

Smiling as if he just found the humor in some bad joke with eyes that refused to overflow with the tears that gathered in the corners, "I was so worried about her all this time that I never considered that she just didn't want to deal with me."

He actually looked like he was in pain. As if he had been in truth worried. Naomi saw the tears in his eyes.

21 TOXICITY

He was weak. Weak and trifling and too damn pathetic. What in the hell could Kini have seen in him was what she wondered as she looked at him glaring down at the floor looking completely emasculated. Where was all this pain when Kini was sitting home waiting on him all those nights? Naomi wondered if he had thought about all the nights he had allowed Kini to sit at home waiting on him to find time to squeeze her into his busy life. If he had thought about the nights he had left her to put full course meals in the refrigerator uneaten because he cancelled at the last moment. She thought about the night they all had all gone out to dinner. Couples' night was what Kini had called it in her e-invitation. Seven couples and Yakini sat down to eat that night, her cell phone vibrated and she read a text and went to the bathroom. She came back to the table with smudged mascara telling the table that Kyle's daughter was sick and he couldn't leave her with a sitter. She sat there that night with a smile plastered to her face and ate her appetizer, joked with the rest of the guests throughout dinner, and quickly nibbled her dessert. She left as soon as the check arrived. No one mentioned the awkwardness. She had prepared this night out for a month. She even scheduled it on a night that everyone was free so that her friends could meet the man she had pinned as the one. No one made mention of him during the table talk instead it loomed over the table until she finally paid.

Each couple whispered about how they would never do that to one another, but no one spoke about it aloud. Now he stood here, powerless and lonely. Sad ass was what Naomi thought, karma can be a bitch. But he did look pitiful.

Her girl was definitely one to be missed. For the first three or four days, Naomi had searched for things to occupy her time as she waited on her girl to return home. Finally, she settled on keeping up with the tour for Kini via scrapbook, composed of all the pictures and articles Kini emailed and posted on her social media. In the years that they had been friends, Kini had served as a point of stability the only family connection this side of the states and these last months had been long. The people sitting nearby looked back while the two whispered and Naomi could feel the stares. She put her hand on his shoulder and led him out to the parking lot.

~~~~~~~~~~~~~~

"Look Kyle, I know how you feel. I miss her too."

He looked at her with a critical frown, "Yeah I know, but it isn't the same Na. At least she told you where she was going and you talk to her. She just cut me off. If I didn't run into you tonight, hell I would be at home now leaving another long message that she probably won't even listen to. I don't think I need to bother her when she comes back. She clearly made her choice not to tell me for a reason. She has my number when she wants to talk."

"Just like that you give up? Light switch effect niggas trip me out. So, you can go from being this heartbroken boyfriend to forget that hoe machismo b.s. in one stroke
~~~~~~~~~~~~~~

huh?"

"Don't try to make me the bad guy Naomi. I haven't done shit. This is your girl's issue. I tried."

"Negro please, you put that woman on hold over and over after Paulette moved back. She sat at home so many times crying over your ass that she finally just got plain ass tired. But you didn't miss her until she stopped being available. As long as she was on standby, you didn't worry if a week or a month passed without seeing her. Now you call every day—be honest you don't miss her, you miss being adored and pursued. Giving all that up is hard, but don't sit here crying love all of a sudden; call it what it is, you miss your fan club."

"I have thought about that. I know I took for granted the fact that she would be accommodating. I used her patience…I misused her patience, but Na, I really do miss her. I just wish I could at least talk to her."

"Look Kyle, I know how she felt about you. The girl was for real. She said… well she cared about you a lot is all I can say, but I have something that you might want to see before you talk to her though. I've been working on a scrapbook of her trip. Come by tonight so you can see it."

"It's kind of late. I don't have to bother you tonight."

"Kyle, it's fine. I don't get to sleep until late, never could. But if you can't come then I understand."

~~~~~~~~~~~~~~

He opened the book and browsed the pictures. She looked happy, content in every picture. Standing in front of large lecture halls of students and small crowds at book venues, Kini looked blissful. Naomi saw recognition on his face as he flipped further into the book. Her waist expanded with each passing page. It was a slight change. He knew she liked her clothes fitted, not tight but hugging her curves, but these shirts were loose and billowy. Her face had a new roundness that he never noticed before. He looked at
~~~~~~~~~~~~~~

Naomi for assurance.

"Yeah she is."

He took a breath. She couldn't be. She would have called. She would have said something. There was no way she would leave him and not tell him. Maybe it wasn't his. Maybe she didn't want to deal with telling him that she was with someone else, but he knew that it was. He knew that the small bulge that appeared slowly from picture to picture was somehow connected to him. He looked at the last page and studied her face to find some trace of sadness. Did she miss him? She had to think about him. She carried a piece of him there in that picture a small part of him resided within her and he looked at the pictures with awe.

"How many months?"

"Five, maybe six… I'm, not sure. We talked about it some, but she just mentioned it like she was talking about the weather or something."

Had it really been that long?

The first month or two it didn't seem so bad like another break but five months. He looked at the last picture and the tears welled again. Naomi saw them and tried to ignore the instinct to tell him to stop acting so soft. She fought it off and instead reached her hand to his face and wiped his left eye with her ring finger.

He smiled, and they both thought of how much they needed Kini tonight. Her presence for them both had become more than friend and lover, but stability and sincerity. She gave each what was lacking and tonight as they stared at her journey wishing that she would have allowed them each to come and borrow moments from her life, they found solace within each other. Her finger lingered on his cheek and traveled to the back of his head.

She leaned in to kiss his cheek innocently, but instead her lips grazed his. Initially he pushed her away. They held one another in an awkward embrace. Kini's man laid down his heartache between his lover's friend's legs. He pushed out all the desires he had wished to say to Kini into Naomi's essence. Rested his lonely head on her breasts and sobbed for himself and Yakini and Naomi. Kini's best friend allowed her loneliness to allow her to violate the one person she had. Her codependency needed to be validated and filled. They both released all the energy they had saved over the past months of longing for Yakini's return, they lay together holding on tightly until the morning light came in. She lay completely still as he arose to dress. Her arms tightly cuddled the pillow beneath her head and her face was tranquil.

She looked peaceful too peaceful for him to feel comfortable in the room. He wanted to get away from the room quickly; he wanted to forget the affair, to erase the caress of her skin from his own. He didn't shower didn't even wash his face but quickly grabbed his clothes and headed to the bedroom door. But he couldn't leave. He looked back at the bed at her lifeless body. When he rushed into the house to get dressed for work, Paulette was sitting on the sofa reading the paper. He didn't even look at her, he didn't want any trivial conversations, and he definitely didn't want to listen to her bicker at him for not being available so that she could do some random chore early this morning.

~~~~~~~~~~~~~

She still sat there when he came down, not reading, but sitting as if she were waiting for him to return to the room. He walked past her without a glance to put the coffee pot on. He drank it black. There was no cream in the house, no sugar either, the molasses sat on the counter, but he chose instead to taste the bitter blackness of the Columbian brew he had bought last week. He sipped at the hot liquid, not blowing the cup as he usually did; dazed, he looked at the front page of the paper attempting to make sense of the jumble of letters there.

"I think I may have to go into work today, and Khai has
~~~~~~~~~~~~~

a birthday party to attend."

"I can't today." He could see the look of annoyance on her face. Her eyes squinted together creating small-ridged folds to appear between the two just below her forehead.

"Do you have to work or something?"

"No, I need to get away for a little while is all. Look I never say no when you need me, but today I need some time."

"What does that mean? You said that you would let her stay here anytime I needed to work. You make all these claims then you go and change your mind."

"Paulette, you're full of it, you know. You told me months ago that you were planning to get your own place. You told me you were going to get her put into daycare, you told me that you would help pay some bills, and you even told me that you would tell MY daughter that I am her father. So don't start playing victim here. I give you all my time. I don't ask for a thing in return because that is my daughter and I love her despite of the fact that she has a trifling ass mom. I stay up nights when she's sick even though I am the one who has to go to work in the mornings, I help her with her alphabet and colors and reading. I do, and I do it because I love her. I pushed Yakini to the side for you so many nights, every time you needed me here, I cancelled on her. Every time I was out on a date and you called me I left her wherever we were be it the movies, a party, even mid-dinner. I made her feel like she was second place every time. I am tired of it Paulette. Not today, I can't."

"So you are choosing a woman over your own daughter? Just like a man, you claim you want to be a daddy but only when it is convenient," she was yelling.

He fought himself to keep his fist at his side; he knew that he had to leave soon, "Girl stop, I haven't been out of this house other than to go to work or Harmony for the past three months. You on the other hand are at the club every damn weekend, and I stay here with Khai. I play mommy and daddy and my daughter doesn't even know who I am. I don't feel like arguing, I can't do it today, so call in and tell them you can't make it. I need some time alone today."

"Alone and how are Khai and I supposed to get around today, huh? I know you are not gonna make me ride the bus with her when you have a car."

"How about staying at home, for once?"

Walking out of the room and grabbing the brown shoulder attaché, Kyle began to reflect over her nerve to question his dedication to his child. All the times he'd sat home so that she could go out dancing or even on dates, he had never questioned her love for their daughter. He saw it as her time to finally do all the things he had been free to do while she raised their daughter, but as time passed he wondered how many nights Ivan had sat home waiting on Paulette to get back from the club while nursing his sick daughter.

Hitting a woman was never a justified act but how much stress can a man take, especially a man providing and caring for a child not his own while a woman like Paulette parades around seeking attention from any willing eyes.

He thought, "I bet that man sat home wondering where the hell she was going in that strapless black dress she wears on Friday nights or those tight jeans and stilettos while he waited at home with Khai. Heck, I bet she even used the work excuse on him. The other week she used that one, only when I happened to walk out of the kitchen with a glass of water she was sneaking in with stilettos on instead of nurses' shoes. Ivan probably got sick of her reasons and her stories of going out for a drink after work with the girls. That crap gets old."

He went to work, even though he didn't have a Saturday class and actually had nothing to grade or write, he went in and sat at his computer and stared at the blank Word document. He thought of working on his compilation of poems but redirected the writing instead into a text:

> I talked to Naomi, and she showed me your pictures. Why didn't you tell me? I have thought about you everyday for the past three and a half months and have called you more times that I can count. I even considered calling your mother's but remembered that I didn't have a number or an exact city when I called Information. I haven't given up on us, and I hope when you read this you will consider returning my calls. I can't deal with this again. You know how much I fought to see Khai. I can't have another child that doesn't know me, and I can't not have you in my life. Kini I know I made you feel insignificant. I made you feel unappreciated and put aside, but baby I love you more than I can express. And I know this isn't poetic and it isn't elegant, and I can't try to focus on words and rhymes and rhythms 'cause the hurt is mixing up my words and I want so bad for you to just know that I miss you. I miss you more that I ever thought possible to miss anyone and I have waited for you to come back. I just want us to talk. You don't have to say anything, no explanations. I understand it all. I love you.

He sent it and waited. He waited on the call that he wanted so badly to come. He pulled his phone out of his pocket and checked the signal, checked the ringer, checked his messages four times within twenty minutes and then grabbed his bag and headed for the car. He drove downtown and sat at the park. The spring air was nice, not as hot as Georgia summers. The crowd was sparse. His notepad was empty still. He grabbed his pencil, put it between his teeth, and looked up at the sky.

Damn, she isn't gonna call, he thought. But what could he do. He had called, he had written, now he had to wait on her to decide.

~~~~~~~~~~~~~~
~~~~~~~~~~~~~~

The house was quiet and the lights were off. No television boomed as he walked into the house as it usually did. No cartoons were blaring, no radio humming, no Crayolas on the floor so he sat down. He assumed they were out for the day; hell, she might have finally taken the child to the park on her own for once. If it weren't for his daily journeys to the wood-chipped area where the little girl swung on the swings, Khai would never get fresh air. Her mother wasn't the outdoor type, but he tried to explain that Khai needed that time to release some energy. The argument was not worth the energy so he took it as another form of his penitence for his absence in her life so long ago and took her daily.

By nine, he wondered where they were and went up the room. He found her letter on the small twin bed he had bought to go into the guest room. Ten words were all she left for him: Don't want to burden you anymore. Gone home. – Sorry, Paulette

"Shit." She was so selfish.

He wondered, "How could she consider taking my daughter back to that negro, so she could see him slap her mommy upside the head again? Ivan's had been trying to call her and she knew that he warned her not to come back crying to him. She is just doing this to keep me on a leash. There is no way she went back there after the last time."

But as he thought about it, he knew that she would go back. He knew that she would go because she needed the attention that he was no longer willing to give. Kyle had tried. He wanted to be the father that his daughter needed, but he couldn't be the groupie that Paulette wanted beckoning to her every call and meeting her outrageous demands. He sat on the small bed and buried his head into the little pillow that smelled of baby lotion and grease. He breathed the smell in deep and cried into the picture of the wide-eyed LOL cartoon that stared from the fabric.

He called his voicemail. The monotone voice said, "You have no new messages and one old message."

He waited to hear the ranting of Paulette; instead, he heard Naomi's voice.

"Kyle, look I am sorry about last night. I know that you didn't mean for it to happen. Hell, I didn't either. Don't worry I won't tell Kini. I can't tell my girl that. Look, we can forget it happened ok. Don't tell her. It isn't about you this time. Kini is my family, and if she was to cut me off, I don't know what I'd do. I guess, this message is long. Sorry. Umm. Call her. She needs you. The baby does too. I … I … I guess I just wanted to say that, you know, I'm sorry and um let's just keep it between us."

He knew Paulette had listened. She knew and there was no telling what she might do with the information, but she was gone. He opened the closet hoping to see some indication that they would be back home at least to pack. But it was empty. She had left a pair of sneakers that were too small now and there was a pink bow was in the corner of the closet with a frayed edge and a broken clasp.

"Paulette, I know you listened to the message. Come back home before you do something that you will regret. Don't take Khai back up there. Ivan warned you; didn't he? Hell, when he called your cell he told you that if he saw you he'd kill you. Do you really think Ivan wants to have you come back now, and if you do, it is only a matter of time before he releases his anger on you? She's my daughter too, don't punish her on some bullshit that has nothing to do with her."

Beep the message was too long to finish. Before he could re-record he saw he had a new call coming in. Paulette.

"Hello."

"Paulette where are you?"

"At the bus station. I am going home Kyle. You have enough drama of your own down here. Ivan was just talking, he wouldn't… he'll be happy to have us back. I mean he…he misses me and Khai and I think he learned his lesson… I hope… I don't know where else to go..."

"I'll be there in fifteen minutes to get y'all. Don't get on that bus."

The drive to the bus station seemed longer than the eighteen miles that he knew it was. What if she was gone? He thought about how he would feel to know that he was the reason she put herself back in danger. The parking lot was full and the walk to the door endless. He didn't see her when he scanned the room, but he heard his name in a tiny voice.

"Khai sweetie. You trying to leave me?"

He smiled at her and knew that she had no idea what was going on. She held on to her turquoise book bag and her Bluey coloring book.

"Where is your mommy sweetie?" He knew that Paulette was irresponsible, but there was no way she would leave her child unattended in .la place like this.

"She is sitting right over there." She pointed behind Kyle to the seats by the window.

She didn't look like herself. Her hair was pulled into a ponytail and she wore a gray jogging suit and sneakers. No makeup, no earrings, nothing exhibiting her usual diva style. He walked over and grabbed her bag, and they walked to the car. He remembered the day at the airport when he had picked up Paulette and Khai. The walk to the car was reminiscent of that day. Nothing was said in the car.

At home, he walked Khai to her room and tucked her into bed. After turning on her nightlight, he pulled the door closed and walked back down the stairs where Paulette waited on the sofa.

"You heard it?"

"What part? That you slept with her girl or that you got her pregnant?"

"I guess both."

"Kyle, look I know you don't owe me anything. I'm not your woman, and we're not in a relationship. But the one thing that I have always admired about you is that you've never been like any of the other men I have been with. Kini loves the hell out of you and has put up with a lot since I've been here. How could you do that to her?"

"How do you know what she has put up with? Our relationship hasn't been good for a minute."

"Look Kyle you don't have to explain to me, but she deserves to know."

He looked at her and wondered if her sudden concern was for Yakini's benefit or for his own pain. She was right in a way. Kini did deserve to know some of it, but if he told her then what about the baby.

"Paulette, I know what you mean, but Kini and I haven't spent time together for months, and I will not let our first conversation be me telling her I slept with her girl. What if she takes the baby? Huh, what if she keeps me away?" He shook his head emphatically, "Uh-uh I am not going to do that again. This one I am going to keep."

"The woman or the baby?"

"Both."

22 LIGHT

Initially when she read the email, she wasn't sure if she wanted to call. She had believed him before when he said that he would make time for her, but this was honestly the first time he had taken some responsibility in the turn the relationship had taken, and so she called. She had been praying on this one hard—God had obviously finally gotten the message on the novel although not as soon as Yakini would have liked and not at a more awkward time, but He had answered. Maybe the other prayers had trickled their way to Him, and her long drawn out prayers on a real family had finally been given the yes she had desired.

The moment the cell phone picked up and before he had time to say hello she said his name, "Kyle." She had yearned to say the name so that he could hear it. She had said it in her prayers, in dreams, had said it to her tummy, but she had yearned to hear him say hers back in her ear.

"Kini, sweetie. I'm so glad to hear from you."

"Kyle, I guess I need to tell you something…"

"I already know… and I'm so happy. We need to work on thing Kini. Our family needs us to work on things."

She smiled at the word family. She knew deep down that Kyle was always the one for her. Had always been, and they talked again for hours like they had in the start of things. Yakini had planned to visit him by surprise in the morning. After working things out, she couldn't wait to come home and see him. He wasn't expecting her for another three days but when the last bookstore called to cancel her event, she rushed to exchange her ticket for an earlier flight.

Tonight however, she would go to dinner with her girl. It had been months and Naomi was eager to discuss the baby shower. But at six months, the water and tea that she had had with the meal quickly made its way through her delicate system. As she made her way to the lady's room, she spotted Kyle at the table.

He was there with Paulette and Khai—sitting as a family dressed up and enjoying dinner here when he had told Kini that he would most likely be home tonight—writing he had told her. She watched him as he pointed to the menu, but mostly she watched Paulette as she gazed at the two. Paulette reached up and readjusted a loc that had fallen in his face. He smiled at her. They looked like a family. Kini wondered where she and a baby fit into this picture. He lived with his baby and her mother. They were a family.

She walked over quickly before she changed her mind. The games were tiresome. He was sitting here with his family after just talking to her the night before about buying a new house and getting married. He was where he wanted to be and she was sure that there was no way that Paulette and Khai would be staying with them if they bought another house. Or maybe he would let them stay in his house. She was too tired of taking the back seat in this relationship and she was ready to tell him that she did not need him to pretend to be happy about this new baby. She would be fine and he could stay with his happy little family here at this table eating desserts and smiling and pointing out little pictures on menus. She didn't need him.

Paulette had heard him talking late nights again on the phone, and often lingered at his door as she made her way to the bathroom. Once she saw him scribbling girl's name on a yellow legal pad while drinking coffee and had offhandedly asked if the baby was a girl. He said yes and told her that he had come up with a name for her, Sohni Justice. She knew if she didn't decided soon for Khai to know the truth, it would be too late for her to enjoy him alone—even if only for a little while.

"Which one do you want?"

She watched him as he helped Khai pick out a dessert from the menu explaining what each one was made out of and making sweet faces while she deliberated between chocolate cake and vanilla ice cream drizzled with caramel and covered with chocolate shavings.

He was finally getting his wish to spend the entire day lavishing her with her favorites before revealing the truth to his sweet girl. Paulette had observed him for the past week making the arrangements, making reservations, checking Khai out of school early to spend the entire Friday at the matinee and then off to the game room for hours of video games. This was the last stop and after dessert they would take a horse and buggy ride and he'd whisper the truth in her ear as if it were some special secret.

Watching each moment, Paulette pushed back tears, wishing she had allowed him to tell her earlier. Praying that Khai didn't blame her for the lies she had been made to believe for so long. The pretty lilac dressed and shiny patent leather shoes made her look even more adorable that normal. They sat at the table and ordered dessert. After seeing the twinkle growing in his eyes as he thought of becoming a new father again, Paulette wondered how long would it be before Kyle's need to father was met by a smaller version that the little bundle they had created six years ago.

"Kyle."

Kyle looked up and saw Yakini with her protruding stomach standing with a grimace on her face. He looked at Khai first to see her reaction to the tummy before saying a word. She looked confused at first and then smiled at Yakini and said a shy hello, but Yakini's tight face was focused solely on Kyle.

"Hey Yakini, I thought you weren't coming back for a few more days."

"I thought I would surprise you, but I guess that's your job as usual." Her voice rose slightly with each word.

"Kini what are you talking about. I'm just saying I wasn't expecting to see you, that is…"

"So are you out on a family dinner or what Kyle? I thought you said that you weren't even with her. You said that you both are doing your own things now and that you and Paulette don't even hang out. I asked you if you were trying to work on things. I mean I know you two have a family together and that you love your daughter and that you have to talk sometimes, but what about our baby huh?"

He tried to hush her voice down as the crowd began to stir. She was loud and her voice was cracking as the tears streamed down her face. She thought of the nights she had waited on him only to be told that Paulette needed him to do some random thing or that his daughter wanted him to stay home that night. She refused to be put behind them again. She was tired of being rescheduled as if she were some tooth cleaning that could wait.

"You tell me that you want a family with me Kyle. That we're going to get married and all this fantasy type shit. But I come home and here you are playing family man with your baby's mama and your kid and I come over and get the "Oh hey Yakini" bit from you. You don't even stand up to give me a damn hug. I am tired. I will not take second seat again."

Kyle tried to hush her. To stop the yelling. Khai looked confused and the other tables were staring, but Paulette thought a woman's view might help.

"Kini, we were just out to dinner. He was just trying to have a nice night with his daughter, really, and he asked me if I wanted to come."

"I wasn't talking to you. If it weren't for you coming down here, we would be fine. We would be happy, and I wouldn't have to sit and wonder when it was convenient to see my man. I don't need you to explain anything to me."

"Kini girl, I promise I don't want him. You can have him. I just wanted you to know that we're not here on some kind of date. We just brought our daughter out to eat."

"We were fine until you came. He was with me everyday, you know that, we were happy, we were in love, and we spent all our time together. It's your fault we are not together. You didn't want him remember. I can't believe you are actually trying to explain anything to me… He's mine… You didn't want him then so don't try to break up OUR FAMILY now. I could see your scheming; every time I wanted to see him, you had to think of something to keep him busy. Naomi told me …"

"No you didn't bring that trifling ho into it."

"Who are you calling trifling, she had you pinned. She told me when you first moved down here that things would change she told me you would try to get him back, but I said no I know my man he wouldn't do me like that. She was right."

"Oh that is what your girl said huh? Your girl has your back all the time I bet. I bet she didn't tell you she slept with your man, did she?"

He saw her hand coming toward his face and reached for her arm but missed. The slap on his cheek was hard; he kept his face turned to keep from reacting to her. He heard her walk away, but didn't move. Instead, he kneeled next to Khai who sat crying into her folded napkin, rocking back and forth. He had found her many nights in the corner of her bedroom rocking this way jumbling words about her mom and Ivan and blood. He held her in his arms and called for his check. She pushed him away as he tried to hold her close and whisper the secret into her ear. She didn't move when he finished telling her. In the car, she sat with her face to the window staring into the dark.

23 BREAKDOWNS

That girl can't still be in the restroom I know.

"Could we get a few minutes? My friend went to the ladies room; I need to go check on her."

"Yes Madame, I will come back in a few minutes."

As she walks toward the restrooms, Naomi notices Kyle and Paulette leaving the restaurant.

"I bet he doesn't even know Kini is here," she whispers to herself as she walks over; and then shouts a hello.

"Hey Kyle."

He looks and then looks away without a word. It is awkward seeing him here. But at least I get to see him alone first. His look would have told a story within itself.

"I was just having dinner with Kini. I was just coming over to let you know that she was here is all. I think she's in the bathroom. You should say hi before you go though."

"She left," Paulette looks at Naomi and says the words in a tone that reveals that not only she knows but that Yakini knows too.

"Kyle you didn't."

"He didn't; I did."

The full parking garage is packed with cars but the purple space 147 is empty. With the car gone, Naomi hails a cab, and the ride home is lengthened as Naomi tries to think of a way to tell her girl the truth. On the fourth ring the voicemail answers, and Naomi sobs into the phone. FINALLY, on the seventh call she leaves a message: "Kini, I am so sorry. I know that you know about Kyle. I promise I didn't want to hurt you. It was a mistake and girl I wish I could take it back girl. Please, Kini just call me so we can talk."

~~~~~~~~~~~~~~

The deep red liquid created a sticky mess on her legs and the sheets. The cramps in her stomach were hard. As she reached to get phone on the left-hand night table, another cramp hit and for minutes she waited in the smell of blood that squished in the folds of her nightgown as she groped for the phone.

"God please don't take them both."

The phone rang and his voicemail picked up.

"Kyle please call me back I need you… oh God," her voice trailed off in sobs.

She called again, but Paulette answered, and so she hung up. Yakini dialed again. But Naomi's voicemail picked up, no answer.

The wailing came closer and the red lights emitted light into the room. The florescent lights were bright and her throat, dry. She reached for the glass on the table but the needle in her arm wouldn't let her move to get the glass. In the past two months, motherhood had become a reality. Talking to her tummy, Sohni Justice, had become her newest best friend.

Now, she reached down to caress the swollen belly that has acted as her only friends on the tour. It wasn't the lack of distension that alerted her attention first; rather it was the softness of it. The lacking of tautness. The loose muscles and fat were not the same consistency she has come to know as Sohni. Panicking, she pressed for the nurse. They
~~~~~~~~~~~~~~

came in with masks and gloves on and needles ready. She slept.

~~~~~~~~~~~~~~

I begged Him, but the blood from the bed was my answer. He took her too, premature labor with too little dilatation. Sohni had descended partly and her little neck could not bear both forces that both attempted to expel and keep her at once. Two days of sedation and a bundle of forms were all I had to take home.

Home had been too lonely and quiet. The little clothes sat on the bed futilely waiting on an owner that would never arrive. The silence was unsympathetic and although Naomi had betrayed me, there was no other place I wanted to go. I knocked slowly. Waiting to hear the sound of heels clicking onto the foyer. But they did not come. I dug in my purse to get my key. The sound of water pervaded the house.

"NaNa, girl where are you?"

Dishes sat on the counter. I guess I'll straighten this up while I wait. Mothering Naomi has become second nature. In college, my room was a mess on the weekends that Naomi visited home. Dishes went unwashed, beds unmade, and clothes never folded.

"NaNa, are you coming out or what?"

Knocking on the door, it opens slightly. The floor is covered in red water. The blood has coagulated on her wrists. The water pours out of the spout and streams red waves onto the floor. A piece of yellow paper sits on the toilet neatly folded with my name on it:

My muse went on homage leaving my mind to wait
The soul my muse's lover also waits patiently
To lay with her and copulate generations of ideas
Yet she stays away meditating and praying
Refusing our summons
Tempting my mind and the soul to disregard her
~~~~~~~~~~~~~~

Move on to new infatuations
My muse went on homage
She left in the middle of the night
Following bright Venus to Eden's gates
Where she sips from the Euphrates
Bathing her brown skin the sun's rays of light
My mind and the soul sit and ponder their fate
For they always follow my muse
Watching the sway of her hips and tracing the curves of her lips with pencils
Drawing out her features in elongated sentences
Swirling in poetic phrases and rhymes
Now we sit and wait
Waiting on her arrival with exciting tales of afar
We sit and debate whom she loves more
Unknown to us that she loves neither
Narcissism swells in her bosom as she bathes in the Nile
Caressing her arms with Frankincense
Yet my mind and the soul are consumed in passion
We Wait
Sit
Pray for her return

~~~~~~~~~~~~~

"So he's the one?"

"I think so."

"I really am happy for you Kini, just take your time. Like my grandma used to say, 'Don't fall in love too deep girl you just might hurt your self when you land'."

"There you go again. Pessimist."

"Realist."

"Whatever."

This conversation went through Naomi's head over and over and over. Simple. They had had more interesting ones before and after, but this conversation was the one prodding Naomi the night in the bathtub sitting with the razor that
~~~~~~~~~~~~~

was normally used to keep her arched brows nicely shaped. This was the conversation that made her experience so much guilt after having betrayed her best friend by luring in her one to lie down in a bed of deceit. This conversation was the one that made her feel dirtiest when she thought of Kyle's lips on her lower abdomen trailing kisses down her thighs and then slowly, gently, almost lovingly placing himself into her.

As she lay in the ruby bath, she thought of Kini and how her friend sounded when she made the claim that Kyle was her one, and as Naomi heard the small giggle of her friend's voice like a giddy teenager as her girl ended her declaration of love. Naomi also heard the sound of Kyle's breath in her ear as he said Yakini's name over and over in her ear while they both attempted to use each other to gain some sense of Yakini's presence during her absence. They corrupted friendship and love, distorted them into sex and lust and sweat and saliva, and as they uttered one another's name, it was for Yakini that they both yearned.

She thought of this betrayal with each incision on her slender wrist each slice made her think that she was sanctifying herself, eradicating her sin by bleeding it out, purging promiscuity, making her conversion from whoredom to virtuousness in a baptism of blood, her body her only holy sacrament praying for redemption in a pool of her private holy water. She used her body as her vessel of salvation and prepared her sacrificed in hopes that her friend would witness and acknowledge that her intentions were never to hurt her.

Or were they? Did she secretly want to hurt Kini and make her feel the way she had felt since the first day her cousin came to her while the others were outside and slid his hand down the front of her cotton shorts and wiggle his finger between the folds of her small vagina? Maybe she did want her friend to hurt, to know that no woman deserved to be truly happily loved by one man. So Naomi resolved to showed her girl that her man was as fallible as all the others and that like all the other men that Naomi had ever known and come into contact with that he too would yearn to touch the moist warm space between her thighs and that Yakini's was no special prize. She wanted Yakini not to be sad, not to be hurt, but not to be so happy through this man.

Naomi could not see her friend happy, not with a man, because that would mean that she would leave. And then Naomi would be alone to deal with the memories and pains of the cousin who would come and put his lips on her small budding breasts not breasts even but knots on her six-year-old chest, and she could not not have Yakini to call on those nights when she could not escape the dreams. She needed Yakini to be alone and to need her so that she was not alone. So, she seduced her best friend's man to lie down his heartache between her thighs and rest his lonely head on her breasts and sob for himself and Yakini and Naomi after they both released all the energy they had saved over the months of longing for Yakini's return.

~~~~~~~~~~~~~

The phone rang and rang and rang and rang and rang until he finally picked up.

"She's dead."

"Who"

"I called her yesterday."

"What are you talking about?"

"Dead. I'm looking at her now."

"What… what are you talking about?"

"I found her. I was coming to tell her, to see her; I had to tell her about the baby."

"Kini, you aren't making sense."

"I know. I asked Him to let me keep all of you. Mama said if I just ask He'll answer"

"Who'll answer?"

"God."
~~~~~~~~~~~~~

What… what happened to the baby? And who's dead?"

"She is. But I get it now."

"Are you joking? After what happened, you have the nerve to call with riddles? But it's always about Yakini right?"

"Yes," the phone is quiet too quiet, "that's what I fially figured out. . . He did answer me. . . all my mixed-up questions were always posed like they were about big things—but it was always just about me."

"What are you talking about?"

"I asked Him for time to myself… I asked Him to give me some time to just DO ME. So he did. . ."

"Kini. . ."

"I should have called her. But when she called me the other night it was still just me, was always about me. With Nelia, with NaNa, with you. . . it was always about what I wanted. . .what I needed. . . about me. I didn't want to talk to her so I hung up. Then I woke up and the blood was everywhere. I looked at my bed and the blood was everywhere and I didn't know why, but now I see it now. I can't have life be all about ME without giving up all of you—like I did Nelia… She's gone too. You know I sent her to my mom. . . you fought for yours—I gave mine away."

"What are you talking about Kini?"

"I called my mama from the hospital, but nobody was home… so I called Na but she wouldn't answer. I called and I needed her, and I called but she didn't answer because I didn't answer when she needed me. And it was yours to keep and I asked Him to give ME time… so He did and I bled and the blood was everywhere. And now it's on her face and hands. It's on her floor. I called her and she didn't answer and I needed her and she's dead and I need to tell her that I need her so bad but she won't listen to me. Dead they are dead, baby dead, Naomi dead, blood in my pants, and on the bed, and in the water, on the floor."

"Where are you, Kini? Where?"

"In the bathroom. Maybe she's just sleep."
"Where?"
"By the tub."
"Your house?"
"No."
"Naomi's?"
"Yes."

~~~~~~~~~~~~~~

Paulette didn't have to ask who it was about. She could see the look on his face when he had answered. It was Kini. Paulette knew that she would no longer be the damsel that Kyle would run to rescue. But she thought she had a few more months before he would be called on his chivalric duty... no his fatherly duties. But it wasn't time. Maybe Kini had had second thoughts on things and decided it better to forgive Kyle and work things out before the baby was born than to hold a grudge and deal with it later. He hung up the phone and frantically patted his pockets for his keys.

"They're on the kitchen table. Is everything ok with Kini?"

"No...I don't know..."

"Where is she? She's fine, right? Right?"

"I don't know. She's at the hospital."

She could see the look of contempt on his face as she thought about making an attempt to interject her opinion. Things had been beyond tense since the restaurant.

"I hope everything's ok."

She watched him back quickly out of the driveway, heard the screech of wheels as he pulled away. And as she watched him fly down the short street and turn quickly at the stop sign without so much as a yield, she knew things would never be the same again.

~~~~~~~~~~~~~~

Her voice was small and her plea was real for the first time…not about herself for once. She cried out to Him, "God, can You hear me?" She yelled as she stood looking at the ceiling. "I get it… I get it… it can't be just about me… I get it… can we start over… I'll get it right this time… I promise… I know it can't be just me now… Let him stay for me and for Nelia and for him too. He needs me too. I get it now. I finally see it now."

~~~~~~~~~~~~~

"She's been like this for days now Mr. Niane. When we got to her house, the baby had fully descended and Yakini was unconscious. But she's been awake since Saturday. We keep telling her there isn't any blood anymore. We even rolled the baby in the room once, but we couldn't let her keep the baby like this… Ms. Johnson's parents are down in the nursery, and her other daughter's staying with a friend, Naomi I think. Anyways we were told to call you."

She looked completely dazed. Those eyes seemed so far away now and nothing in them looked like the woman he knew.

He whispered in her ear, "Kini, I'm here."

The eyes were blank and seemed to be so removed from the world that he lived in, but he knew she was in there somewhere. He sat on the bed, and leaned her head on his chest.

~~~~~~~~~~~~~

The room was bright when she opened her eyes, but the water wasn't running anymore. She looked up slightly and saw that beautiful smile rise like a dawning sun, it just slowly rose upward until his lips slightly curved, parted slightly, and the smile was as phenomenal as the sun.

He finally heard me, He finally heard me. And the sun of Kyle's smile filled the room and her heart, and her faith rekindled slowly and glowed to match his smile.

ABOUT THE AUTHOR

Kirsten Geter is an author known for her captivating and insightful works. A poet for over two decades, an owner of a collaborative publishing company, and a George Washington Carver Educator Award winner, Geter has also written various genres such as short stories, essays, and her previous memoir, "Seven Days of Living While Single".

Geter creates vivid descriptions and evokes profound emotions setting her apart as a skilled storyteller. The interludes of poetry scattered throughout her last novel enhance the narrative, immersing readers in a world where language becomes a gateway to the soul.

Quiet Revisions delves into the human condition, love, and the enduring impact of artistic expression.

With each page, Geter's poetic prose resonates, leaving a lasting impression on readers' hearts and minds.

Kirsten Geter's remarkable storytelling and her ability to touch the core of the human experience make this novel a must-read for enthusiasts of literary fiction.

www.ingramcontent.com/pod-product-compliance
Lightning Source LLC
LaVergne TN
LVHW091144080826
845145LV00008B/2257

* 9 7 8 0 9 7 9 4 0 3 2 3 1 *